****

A Grease Junkie's Rags

A Secondhand Homicide Whodunit

Book 3

Myrl V Williams

Back Porch Literature

****

Myrl V Williams

Myrl V Williams

authormyrlvwilliams@gmail.com

Cover Design By: Melody Buntemeyer

Melodybuntemeyer@gmail.com

Myrl V Williams

In loving memory of my dear friend, Kenny Mayeux.

Thank you to JoAnne and Lisa for inspiration and your loyal friendship.

Thank you to Helen for all her love and support.

Myrl V Williams

1

I had my mother to thank for my affinity and love of garage saleing and antiquing. She'd developed it into a weekend ritual since I was old enough to walk, loading my sister and I into the car for an all-day affair which included a cooler with sandwiches and drinks, and a thermos full of hot black coffee for her.

Never underestimate the power of a woman with a newspaper, a map, and a wallet full of small bills on a Saturday morning. My mother could barter with the best of them, a skill I'm proud to have picked up from her.

My younger sister, Darla, detested these outings because she has a severe aversion to antiques and 'old' things. I believe the scientific term for her irrational fear is 'epiplaphobia'. She didn't have an aversion to the ice cream which awaited us at the end of each trip, however. So, her complaining was usually kept to a minimum, lest she endure the wrath of our mother, Linette, who could stifle us with just a look.

Many times, Darla chose to wait in the car with a coloring book and crayons instead of perusing for the treasures my mother and I found so endearing. She would grumble in the backseat, in a voice only I could hear, while my mother bopped her head to some tune on the AM radio.

The warm spring weather had people in town opening garage sales up much earlier than normal for Colorado Springs. Temperatures, which were usually in the 30's and 40's, were up into the mid 60's, highly unusual for this time of year. April showers bring May flowers. In Colorado, this usually meant snow showers and not rain. So, I, along with the rest of the city, was enjoying and taking advantage of the wonderful spring weather.

I donned a jacket over my sweater and jeans, knowing I could shed it later if the temperature rose even further. Dressing in layers is an absolute Colorado must. You never knew when the weather would take a turn for the worse or the better, so one could never truly be prepared. "If you don't like the weather in Colorado, wait an hour"; it was a famous saying the locals touted frequently, especially to tourists.

Climbing into 'the Beast', I set my sights forward to a day of garage sales from the south side (in Security) to the north side (in Briargate), with several stops in between. Of course, my first stop was at the drive-thru coffee kiosk on Powers Blvd. After ordering a white chocolate mocha and a chocolate croissant, I was on my way this gorgeous Friday morning. I texted my business partner, Helen, to let her know I'd be scouting out items for our vintage boutique, The Back Porch on Bijou.

I am a huge Eagles fan, the band, not the pro football team (I am a diehard Broncos fan down to my soul, my family bleeds orange and blue). My dog, Peyton, is even named after one of the best quarterbacks the NFL has ever seen.

So, when I saw the t-shirt on a hanger at the third stop on my map, I knew I had to have it. It was XXL, making it perfect for sleeping in and reliving my youth. This was one item I'd be keeping for myself and not saving for the shop.

This t-shirt was a classic. I mean, a 1974 Eagles Tour original was hard to come by, and considering it was forty plus years old, it was in mint condition, no stains, no tears, near perfection. These people obviously didn't realize what a little gem they had hanging there, and I didn't plan on making them any the wiser. I paid for it as well as several other items I thought I could resell or repurpose for the shop, then went on my merry way.

Making the rounds of all the places I had jotted down in my handy dandy notebook; I was finally ready to head back to the hacienda, to grab a quick bite and let Peyton, my loving, little shih tzu and loyal companion, out to stretch his legs and take care of any other business he required, before heading downtown to the shop.

Once home, I kicked off my shoes and dialed up my favorite pizza joint, placing my order for delivery.

While I waited, I stripped out of my sweater and jeans to try on my new find. Slipping it over my head and extending my arms into the sleeves, I made a gnarly air guitar move. Wwhrrrrrraunnnngggggg! I let my fingertips reverberate on my imaginary strings. A sudden pain in my right hand led me to gaze down upon my throbbing appendage. These fingertips and fingernails were stained black with grease and grime. It was then I realized I wasn't the only would-be air guitarist who'd worn this shirt.

Finding myself in some dimly lit place, I tried to get my bearings as I rubbed at the pain in my swollen right hand. It appeared to be a garage of some sort because I could see three sets of huge glass garage doors. Through the doors, I could make out traffic rolling by on the street outside. Looking down, I noticed a deep hole in the floor behind me, which I recognized as a grease pit.

"I warned you, you're either with me or you'll suffer the consequences," came a raspy voice from the shadows.

"I told *you*; I'm not getting involved with you," these were words I heard myself ushering forth in a young man's voice. "Just leave me alone."

"And I told *you*, you didn't have a choice. I always get what I want."

The figure approached menacingly, at a steady pace. It was too dark inside the garage for me to make out the figure clearly. I took a step back. Recollections of my stumbling fall, on the ice, over a year ago flooded my memory, as I found myself teetering precariously at the edge of the grease pit. Horror raced through my head as the figure pushed me in the chest with two fingers, sending me plummeting backwards into the pit. My arms flailed wildly as I fell, the ceiling rushing away from me, like something out of a science fiction movie.

Frantically, I grabbed at the air trying to grasp anything to stop or slow my descent, panic engulfing my every thought. The breath burst from my lungs with the sudden impact of slamming into the concrete below. My head slammed into the floor, generating a ripple through the muscles in my neck and down my spine. Then there was a nothingness which surrounded me in a shroud of darkness.

I peeled the shirt off in a flash, leaving me standing there trembling in my bra and panties. Tossing it on the bed, I groaned and stared at it, now lamenting my purchase. In my younger days, I'd had fantasies about stripping down in front of Don Henley, but this was a bit too much, even for this Eagles groupie.

On the verge of tears, I plopped onto the floor and sat cross legged, leaning back against the foot of my bed, banging my head into the soft mattress several times. I was not ready to do this again. I sat there bemoaning my recently acquired paranormal endowment, one I would gladly relinquish if I had the slightest idea of how.

You would think I'd be used to this, since this was the third time it had happened to me, but I *still* could not wrap my head around the idea of suddenly being thrust into someone else's mind. Especially when that someone else was no longer a living, breathing member of functioning society. It still creeped me out, in a major kind of way. I wasn't sure I'd ever get used to this.

Still in a state of shock when my pizza arrived, I asked the driver to just leave it at the door. Now, not being in the mood to nosh on pepperoni and cheese, I slipped the box into the oven to save it for later.

An hour later, when I'd finally composed myself, I put my clothes back on so I could take the shirt downtown to Homicide Detective Jace Kendall. I wasn't sure how he'd receive me. It had taken some convincing to get him to believe in my newly acquired paranormal ability.

This would be the third time I would be visiting his office down at the Colorado Springs Police Department. I still wasn't sure if I really liked the man. He had this irksome habit of smirking at you in such a condescending manner, which I found utterly annoying and agitating. With his young age and youthful looks, I had taken to calling him The Boy Child Detective.

2

Under the cloudless blue Colorado sky, I pulled into the parking lot of the brick façade which was the Colorado Springs Police Department (CSPD). I took my time walking into the building, prolonging my inevitable visit with Kendall.

Officer Jenkins waved me through. He always seemed to be the one on duty whenever I needed to see the boy child detective.

"Is it still warm out there, Ms. Windsor?" He inquired, with a pleasant smile.

"It's gorgeous, Officer Jenkins, almost sixty-eight degrees out there. But I hear we're in for a snowstorm on Sunday."

"We could use the moisture, that's for sure."

In Colorado's arid climate, we were never averse to rain, sleet, or snow, we drew the line at hail. But if said snow had caused you to acquire a freaky paranormal ability, you may be averse to snow as well. A fall on a snow-covered sidewalk last year had done just that to me and I was not relishing it in the least.

“Yes, we could,” I confirmed, as he greeted the next person who had walked in.

I collected my belongings after putting them through the metal detector and turned towards the sign pointing me in the direction of the Major Crime Division.

Making my way through the labyrinth of corridors, and up the elevator, I weaved my way to Homicide, not really looking forward to another visit with the CSPD detective.

I knocked on the door to Det. Jace Kendall’s office. Without looking up, he waved me in. From the scowl on his face, I could tell he wasn’t in the greatest of moods and seeing me usually made his mood even worse. But here I was…

“Just leave the report on my desk,” he said in an undertone, pointing to the right corner of his workspace, indicating a huge pile of paperwork there.

I cleared my throat and Kendall looked up.

“Oh, no,” he groaned, his shoulders slumping forward.

"It's nice to see you too, detective," sarcasm dripping from my words.

"You being in my office… can only mean trouble for me."

A fake smile lit up my face and I flirtatiously batted my eyelashes. "Maybe, I'm here to ask you out."

He let out a loud humph. "I know I'm going to regret this, but what brings you into my office today?"

Reaching into my bag, I pulled out the Eagles t-shirt and held it up for him to see.

His eyes narrowed. "Do you go looking for these items? Or do they just fall into your lap?"

"Of course I go looking for the items. I own a vintage shop, but I don't specifically go looking for items previously owned by murder victims if that's what you're asking," I admitted. "That part… that part just falls into my lap."

Putting his hands over his face, he shook his head.

"I kinda have a full plate right now," he complained, raking his fingers down to his chin and then pointing to a stack of thick folders on his desk.

"Well, I've already solved a couple of murders for you. I suppose I could solve this one too," I replied, giving a one shouldered shrug.

A heavy sigh and menacing glare were directed towards me.

"Fine, tell me about the shirt," he groaned begrudgingly and stared back down at his desk.

"I don't know anything about the victim except he was pushed into one of those pit things in a mechanic's shop…"

It was all I was able to get out.

"You're kidding, right?" He looked up quickly, consternation marking his young face.

"Kendall, I wouldn't joke around about something as serious as this. We're talking about murder here."

"I… could kiss you right now!" Kendall beamed.

I wrinkled my brow, and turned to leave, pointing at the door, I uttered, "Umm, maybe I should come back another time."

He jumped up from his chair as if someone had lit a fire beneath his behind. Rushing around the desk, he grabbed me by my shoulders.

"This is one of the things on my plate," he explained, squeezing my shoulders tighter.

I stared blankly. He gave my shoulders a little shake.

"Two years ago, we were called to a mechanic's shop on Platte Avenue, Big Al's Automotive. The body of a 19-year-old boy, named Dax Rubins, was discovered in the grease pit when the shop opened. His death was suspicious to me, but it was ruled an accident. It was assumed he had slipped and fallen but there was no oil found on the kid's shoes, but my gut says he was pushed. I keep going over it trying to find any evidence to prove it was a homicide. Everything leads to a dead end. It's one of the cases I'm working on."

"Maybe I *can* help then," I offered hopefully.

"Yeah, maybe. I could use a break in this case. Something about his death just never set right with me."

He hadn't released the grip he had on my shoulders yet and I was beginning to feel uncomfortable with the lack of space between the two of us.

"You're not going to kiss me, are you?"

A sly smile formed on his lips, and he gave me a one eyed Elvis look. "Do you want me to?"

I pulled back, leaning away from him. "Uh, no."

"You sure?" He grinned even broader.

"Yes," I nodded, "I'm quite sure."

He chuckled and let go of me.

Phew, I thought I was going to have to smack the boy child detective there for a minute.

"Where'd you get the shirt?" He asked, taking a seat behind his desk again.

"I found it at a garage sale over off of Chelton. Imagine my surprise when I put it on, only to find myself in a dark garage and then being pushed into the pit thing in a mechanic's shop. I don't think I've ever stripped out of my clothes as fast as I did."

A huge grin stretched from ear to ear.

"I bet that was a sight to see," he quipped, the grin glowing across his face.

I rolled my eyes and shook my head.

"Can we get back to the case at hand, please?"

He held up a finger.

"Give me a minute," he insisted and closed his eyes.

I watched another grin spread across his boyish face and then an audible snicker escaped his chest. He was incorrigible.

"Are you quite finished?" I asked, exasperation seeping from my soul.

He opened his eyes and gave me a quick nod. "Done."

Gritting my teeth, I glared at him. "Do you want to know about this shirt or not?"

His face took on a serious tone.

"I do," he replied, waggling his fingers at me in a 'give it to me' gesture.

"Someone was threatening him. He told the person he wasn't going to get involved with them. He was standing at the edge and the person poked him in the chest knocking him backwards into the pit."

"Did he see their face?"

I shook my head. "No, the person threatening him was concealed by the darkness in the garage. There was very little light coming in through the big garage doors and the lights weren't on inside."

"Could you tell what they were wearing?"

"No, sorry."

"There had been rumors of drug activity associated with the place, but they cleaned it up fast, if there was any. We couldn't find anything drug related. We got some hits with the dogs, but if anything had been there it was gone by the time we were called to the shop."

"Well, the boy didn't mention drugs specifically, but he didn't want to be involved with the person who pushed him. Was there any trace of drugs in his system per the autopsy?"

"No, toxicology screen came back clean. Rumors have circulated for the last few years about Big Al running drugs out of his shop. Vice has never been able to prove anything, and everything points to Al being a stand-up guy. Any investigation into his affairs leads nowhere. When I interviewed Dax's girlfriend, she said he had complained to her about someone at work giving him a hard time, but he never elaborated on it with her. There was also another kid named Trent Powers who worked there at the same time…conveniently, he's now engaged to Prentiss Reeves, the girl Dax was dating back then."

Kendall pulled a folder from the stack on his desk and flipped it open. Running his finger down the page, he stopped. "I remember they were inseparable at the funeral. He had his arm around her the whole time. Getting the boyfriend out of the way so he could steal his girl has been a motive for murder for decades."

"Maybe."

He flipped the folder around and tapped a black and white picture of a young woman being consoled by a young man.

"You were at the funeral?"

Kendall nodded. "I was hanging out in the back taking pictures of the crowd. Like I said, I thought it was a suspicious death. The body wasn't discovered or reported until the next day. The owner claimed he had no idea why Dax was there so late. All the other employees told us Dax was still there when they had clocked out."

His eyes returned to me, throwing his hands up. "Why am I telling you this?"

I sighed loudly. "To help me understand what I'm looking for in the vision. The more I know, the better I can try to help you. Give me a couple of days and I'll put the shirt on again and see if I come up with anything for you. I'm just not ready to do it today or probably even tomorrow."

Disappointment reared its head, but Kendall had seen firsthand on the case before, how the items affected me. "I understand. I'll wait for you to call me. And Ms. Windsor…"

"I know, I know," I cut him off, holding my hand up and standing to make my exit. "You'll have me arrested if you find me interfering with your investigation."

He scowled. "So far, that message has yet to sink in with you."

"Yeah, yeah, yeah."

"Ms. Windsor?"

I stopped and turned around in the doorway.

"Yes?"

Kendall peeked around the edge of his desk and looked at my lower body. "By the way, what color of underwear *do* you have on?"

The dreaded smirk was this time accompanied by raised eyebrows.

I glared and shot him a middle finger salute as I turned on my heel and exited, wanting to put distance between us before I said or did something I shouldn't… like smack him in the forehead. There had been several times, since we'd met, in which I'd thought about assaulting this particular police officer, but today wasn't the day for it.

"I know you're just waiting for me to ask you out. It's the reason why you keep coming back to my office," he shouted at my back.

Incorrigible, I tell you.

3

"Where have you been?" Helen asked when I finally arrived at The Back Porch around 2 o'clock.

I stood there numbly and uttered a sigh of heavy exasperation. "I don't know if I can do this much longer."

"Do what? Are you giving up on the shop?" Helen asked in a panic, her face falling and losing all color.

I shook my head, "No, nothing so drastic. I had another vision from a T-shirt I bought at a garage sale this morning. This time it was a 19-year-old boy who was pushed to his death."

At this point, my resolve shattered, and I began to cry uncontrollably. Wracking sobs caused my shoulders to shake violently.

Helen rushed over to me and embraced me in a tight hug. "Oh, Marlie, I'm so sorry."

She held onto me for several minutes before I stopped crying.

"Sit down, I'm going to make you a cup of tea," she commanded.

She left and went into the back while I slumped into the chair at my desk and fumbled for the tissue box to dry my tears and blow my nose. It was what I like to refer to as an 'ugly cry', red eyes and nose, accompanied by sniffles for a good while after. Tissue companies loved 'ugly criers'.

Several minutes later, Helen returned and set a mug of steaming black tea on the desk in front of me.

"I put three spoonfuls of sugar in, just the way you like it. Now, I'm going across the street to get you something to go with your tea," she told me, scurrying out the front door before I could object, not like I had any intentions of truly stopping her.

I'd been trying to cut down on the delectables which Helen and I enjoyed consuming, since one of our clients had asked me out a couple of times. But I do tend to stress eat, so I was excitedly anticipating Helen's return with something sweet and gooey, and hopefully chocolatey.

After about ten minutes, the door tinkled, and a familiar face strolled in behind my business partner. My sister, Darla, was chatting away with Helen. Her face shifted to concern when she looked at me.

“What’s wrong?” Darla asked. “You look like you’ve been crying. You have ‘ugly cry face.’”

“It’s nothing,” I replied numbly, shaking my head, and dabbing at my eyes.

“It isn’t nothing. She’s had another vision,” Helen explained, opening the bag, pulling out a pastry and setting it on a napkin in front of me.

I shot Helen a look with a slight shake to my head.

“What do you mean, she’s had another vision?” My sister inquired, confused and snapping her head in Helen’s direction.

“She doesn’t know about your visions?” Helen asked, casting a thumb in Darla’s direction.

“No, I haven’t told anyone but you. No one knows except you, me, and Kendall,” I admitted. “Oh, and Victoria the mean DA lady.”

"What's going on here?" Darla demanded, placing her hands on her hips indignantly. "Who is Kendall? And what mean DA lady?"

I threw my head back. "Ugh. I keep getting these visions of people's murders when I buy something they owned. Kendall is the cop, down at CSPD, I've been working with, and the district attorney assigned to handle the cases doesn't like me very much. She calls me a fraud. I call *her,* Victoria McNasty. Her last name is McAdams."

Darla looked at me as if I were insane, but I knew what was coming next, so I braced myself for her impending outburst.

"I told you this would happen! How many times did I say it? Why do you think I only buy new things? I don't want spirits attached to anything I own. I'll bet half of the stuff in this place has some sort of ghoul or goblin connected with it," Darla declared loudly, waving her arms around the room.

It hadn't dawned on me, other items in the shop could house latent visions. Most of these things had been collected prior to the fall I'd taken over a year ago. I sat there dumbfounded, my eyes wandering around the room and wondering if she might not be right.

Darla continued, "Have you ever given me anything from the shop as a gift?"

"Uh…nope," I lied, trying to sound convincing, but knowing my sister saw right through me.

"Ah, liar. What did you give me from here?"

"I'm not telling," I answered with a one shouldered shrug, a frown and slight shake to my head.

"I'm just gonna throw out everything you've ever given me then," Darla announced. "And don't plan on giving me a gift ever again."

I had her with her comment.

"Guess I can take Helen with me to the George Strait concert in Denver in August. I bought us tickets for your birthday."

"You did not!"

I opened my desk drawer and pulled out a little white envelope. Removing two tickets to the August concert, I waved them in front of her face.

Clenching her fists and tightening her shoulders, she growled at me.

Helen sat there, watching the conversation bounce back and forth between Darla and me, grinning like a Cheshire cat.

"Oh, it's not the *only* thing she's keeping from you," Helen announced, raising a finger. "She also has the hots for that young homicide detective down at CSPD."

I glared menacingly at Helen. "I do *not* have the *hots* for Jace Kendall."

"Your sister won't admit she's a cougar," Helen told Darla. "She's in denial."

"Don't you have work to do?" I directed towards Helen.

"Nope," she shrugged. "Unlike you, I get here at a decent hour and get my work done in a timely fashion."

Darla rushed over to one of the shelves and picked up an antique vase, then shoved the porcelain vessel into my hands. "This giving off any vibes?"

"Don't be ridiculous," I stated, setting the vase on my desk. But she did have a point. Next time I was alone in the shop though, I was going to have to start investigating as many pieces as I could. Who knew how many other unsolved mysteries were lurking within the items around me? My head was beginning to pound, and I could feel a migraine coming on.

"I'm going home," I announced, grabbing my purse and keys. "I'll leave you two to your deluded fantasies."

"You just got here," Helen challenged.

"If you're leaving, I need you to drop me off at mom's," Darla told me. "I took an I-NAR from the airport to surprise y'all."

"What is an I-NAR?" Helen and I asked in unison.

"It's one of those new ride services. I Need a Ride…I-NAR." Her statement was accompanied by a look and tone which suggested Helen and I needed to get out more.

Looking at one another, Helen and I each gave a shrug.

Wheeling her suitcase behind her, my sister followed me outside, donning sunglasses reminiscent of something sported by Elton John in the 70's.

Darla and I piled into the Jeep and headed towards my parents' house in the middle of town.

"You know I'm going way out of my way to take you to mom and dad's," I protested.

"Yes, I know and thank you," she responded, turning to look out of the window.

I turned over the ignition and seethed inwardly.

"So, you're a cougar?" Darla asked as we pulled out of the driveway and onto Bijou Street a moment later.

"No, I am *not* a cougar," I shouted.

"But you *want* to be a cougar?" My younger sibling continued.

"When did you say you're leaving again?"

Darla offered up a big cheesy grin. "You're stuck with me for two weeks."

"God help me. And don't mention my visions to mom and dad," I warned.

"What's this vision business about any way?"

"About a year ago, I fell and hit my head on the ice. Ever since then, I have bought a few things that when I put them on, they show me the previous owner's murder."

"That is *just damn* creepy."

"You don't have to tell me. I get to live it out."

"So how does it work? You slip into a trance or something?"

"Something like similar," I nodded. "I'll put an item on and then suddenly find myself as the victim, then relive their murder. It's pretty gruesome sometimes, but I'm starting to get used to it now, I guess."

"How many times has this happened?"

"This is the third time. I bought a classic '74 Eagles Tour t-shirt at a garage sale this morning. Come to find out it belonged to a 19-year-old boy who was murdered a few years ago in a mechanic's shop over on Platte."

"I'd quit buying used crap if I were you," she mused. "An authentic '74 Eagles? Great find by the way. I just bought the album in a shop in Nashville a few weeks ago. I love the artwork on the cover, has a very southwest feel to it. Cost me a pretty penny, I'll tell ya."

My sister was diagnosed with Attention Deficit Disorder (ADD) when she was in her thirties. She can change subjects in the blink of an eye and then be back to the first one just as quick. Following her train of thought, was like watching a pinball machine at times.

"Yes, authentic. I had planned on using it as a sleep shirt and dreaming about my man, Don. And you know I love all this old 'crap' as you call it."

"Even if you have to deal with this vision stuff? No thank you," she told me, shaking a finger at me. "You can have Don; you know I always preferred Glen."

Arriving at my parents' home, Darla opened the car door and got out. She pulled her suitcase from the back seat, then stood in the driveway.

"Aren't you coming in?" She asked.

"No, I had dinner with mom and dad last night. I'll let them fawn over you privately for a few hours. You need the attention more than I do, since I'm mom's favorite. And besides, I have to get home before this headache becomes a full-blown migraine."

"In your dreams, I'm mom's favorite," she sneered, slamming the back door of 'the Beast'.

A moment later, my mother opened the front door and came rushing down the steps to greet my sister.

"You didn't tell me your sister was coming," my mother scolded me, taking Darla into an embrace, while Darla gave me a squinty-eyed smirk.

Mid-hug, I asked my mother, "Mom, who's your favorite?"

"I don't have a favorite," my mother denied, releasing my sister.

"That's not what you told me last night," I teased.

My mother waved her fingertips across her neck a few times.

"Oh my Gawd, you did say it," Darla bellowed indignantly, her mouth wide open.

My mother doubled over holding her stomach, irritating Darla even further. "She likes old things, you don't," my mother quipped with a one shouldered shrug and went into the house.

"Told ya," I grinned and stuck my tongue out at my sister.

"Whatever," she sneered.

She picked up her luggage and followed my mother inside, stomping her feet as she went up the front steps.

Irritating my younger sister… will never get old, no matter how old we get. It's what I live for.

Driving home was torture. Both because of the horrendous traffic and because I could feel the migraine building inside my throbbing skull, sure something was going to burst from my forehead at any minute. In my haste to leave the shop and Helen's manic ravings, I'd left my sunglasses on my desk, so squinting to keep the glare out of my eyes didn't help.

Opening the door to the apartment, I was greeted by the yips and yaps of my little shih tzu, Peyton, his tail wagging uncontrollably. He had been a gift from Darla after my divorce so I didn't have to be alone when my son went off to college in Boulder.

I threw the t-shirt onto the chair in the living room then went to get my migraine meds and some water. Sitting on the couch, I downed the horse pills and the water then stared at the t-shirt.

"Why? Why couldn't you just be a regular old t-shirt? Why did you have to be… a death shroud," I snarled at it.

Lying down on the couch, I closed my eyes and let the medication I took begin to work. Three hours later, I awoke feeling like I had cotton in my mouth. A side effect of my migraine medication. Yuck!

My stomach growled and I could hear the pizza I'd ordered for lunch calling my name from its place inside the oven.

"I'm coming, my beautiful little morsel. Coming to devour you."

Peyton sat there staring at me, his tail wagging in anticipation.

"Yes, you can have my crust," I assured him.

Taking the box from the oven, I put two pieces into the air-fryer, a Christmas gift from my son, who claimed it the best invention since… ever… and declared it the best way to reheat cold pizza. He hadn't been wrong on either count as far as I was concerned.

Turning the television on, I couldn't help but to keep looking in the direction of the t-shirt. Not wanting to relive Dax's fall any time soon, I punched the off button on the remote.

Peyton and I went for a quick walk for him to take care of his personals and then returned to the apartment. Ignoring the garment on the back of the chair, I proceeded to the bedroom and changed into my pajamas. A wave of sadness washing over me, knowing I'd never get to sleep in my beloved t-shirt.

Looking down, I declared loudly, "Red, Kendall. I have red underwear on."

4

I'd come in early to test Darla's theory concerning other items inside the shop possibly holding the visions of other murder victims. I was moving from place to place, picking up and handling every item I could, desperately praying no new visions would pop up, not sure I could handle more than one murder at a time. So far, so good!

Hearing a car drive up, I looked out the side window on my tippy toes, to see Helen had just pulled in. Not wanting her to think I was mentally off my rocker, (not that she already didn't, I mean she knew me better than anyone), I put the Autumn Leaf butter dish I was holding back on the shelf, hurried over to my desk and plopped into my chair, busying myself at my computer.

The front door tinkled as Helen walked in, carrying a familiar lavender box.

"You're here early," she remarked, eyeing my desk.

I could smell the deep-fried dough from where I sat and stretched my neck upward, inhaling the deliciousness, hoping there was a bear claw with my name on it in the box.

"What are you doing over there?" My business partner asked me suspiciously, craning her neck in my direction.

"I'm trying to find information on Dax Rubins, the kid who was murdered down at the mechanic's shop," I threw out, manufacturing an excuse on the spot, for my early arrival.

Setting the box down on her desk, along with her purse and day timer, Helen moved towards me.

"Get out of the way," she commanded with a few flicks of her wrist.

Being she was much better at this than I was, I slid back and gave her ample room at my keyboard. Casually maneuvering towards the soft purple box on *her* desk.

Helen's fingers danced daintily across the keyboard and with a click, several articles popped up on my screen.

"There you go," she beamed, giving me a smile dripping with smugness.

"Some days, I just hate you," I told her with a huff, taking a bite out of the gooey bear claw I'd snagged.

"I know," she replied and sat down at her own desk, dipping her hand into the pastry box.

Most of the articles were from our local paper, The Gazette. The first was about his death at Big Al's Automotive Shop. The second relayed information about the day of his funeral. The others were from the sports section. Dax Rubins had been a very popular young man, graduating from Palmer High School with honors and he had been an all-star quarterback for The Terrors.

I clicked on the first article, Local Star Athlete Dies in Accident. There was a picture of Dax, which I assumed to be his graduation picture, as well as one of Big Al's with an ambulance and the coroner's car out front, followed by an article telling of Dax's death after an accidental fall into one of the grease pits.

It's odd how seeing the picture of the victim impacted me. I'd seen Rose O'Brien's reflection in a mirror and there was a picture of Pastor Hawkins at his home. But seeing the picture of a young man before he'd been able to live his life was a different feeling altogether. It left me feeling sad and depressed.

The second article dated a week later showed a picture of the crowd which had amassed at Evergreen Cemetery for the boy's funeral. Members of the football team served as pallbearers and the cemetery was inundated with flowers. According to the article there had been over one-hundred mourners who attended the gravesite services.

"I need to get into that shop," I told her, opening the box and taking out a second bear claw, which I knew I'd regret later. "Kendall says they haven't had any new leads to be able to obtain a search warrant."

Helen tapped her fingers to her lips.

I could see the wheels turning… wait for it.

She pursed her lips.

Patience.

"You could always drain the oil on your car some and then take it in for an oil change at Big Al's," she suggested. "Maybe you'll see or overhear something useful to Kendall."

I'll never let her know it, but the woman is a genius.

"You change your own oil anyway, so you already know what to do," she finished.

The bell on the door tinkled and my sister came waltzing in, swinging her purse in her hand.

"Good morning, peeps," Darla beamed in greeting, "What are the two of you up to?"

"I'm helping your sister with her latest investigation," Helen answered. "I have to make sure she gets her cougar fix. Her hot young detective will most likely have something to say about her snooping around."

"What makes you think Jace Kendall is hot?" I asked, snapping a glance at her through narrowed eyes.

"I looked up his picture on the internet," Helen confessed and then fanned her face with her fingers. "Ooooo, baby."

Darla sat on my desk and bit into an apple she'd pulled from her oversized bag.

"I need to meet this hot detective," she cackled, swinging her feet like a child, and grinning like a fool.

"I'm ignoring the two of you," I told them.

"See how she avoids talking about him?" Helen asked Darla.

"I see that," my sister answered, then directed a question to me. "Why is that?"

"I'm not avoiding your question; I'm ignoring it because it's absurd," I told them, then to my sister, "You know, *you* should become a cop,"

"Why would I want to be a cop," Darla protested.

"Don't know why you wouldn't. You chase the same men they do. You may as well get paid for it," I teased.

"You're an a-hole."

"I'm thinking it will be noisy in the shop. How will I be able to listen in on what's going on there?" I asked, still ignoring their derangement.

"Sneak in and borrow the hearing thingy dad uses to watch TV," Darla suggested, taking another bite from her apple.

This was also a brilliant idea; again, however, I would never let my sister know this. Call me spiteful.

After visiting for about half an hour, Darla left to take my mother shopping and then to lunch.

It was a slow morning at The Back Porch, so I left Helen to greet our customers and went to sabotage the Jeep.

I pulled the big white beast into the side driveway, donned an old raggedy shirt from the storeroom and shimmied under the Jeep; flashlight, and oil pan in hand.

After the 'ex' left, I learned a whole slew of useful skills I never thought I'd need until there was no one around to handle them: changing the oil, changing a tire, jumping a dead battery…among other things.

"Marlie?" I heard a voice call my name. I wiggled out from under the car to find Artie Watters standing there, in khakis and a light blue button-down shirt, ironed and creased in all the right places, immaculate as usual.

He offered me a hand and pulled me to my feet wrinkling his nose as he looked at his now greasy palm. I handed him the rag I had tucked into my back pocket. He wiped his hands and handed it back to me.

"*What* are you doing?" He asked with disdain.

"Changing my oil and oil filter," I smiled, telling my white lie.

"Why on earth would you be changing your own oil?"

"Because it needed to be changed," I sighed in irritation.

"Why not take it to a shop and have it done by professionals?"

"I have better things to spend money on than an oil change. It's not difficult. I've done it several times."

"You are filthy," he told me, scrunching up his face in disgust.

"Well, it's what happens when you crawl around beneath the car I suppose," I remarked with an exaggerated faux smile.

He leaned in as if to kiss my head but then thought better of it, pulling his hands up like he touched something foul. "I'll pick you up later for dinner."

"I promise I'll be presentable," I replied with a bow.

"I dearly hope so. I will be at your apartment at six o'clock."

A strained look crossed his brow, and he left me in my grease-stained mess. Quite frankly, I was shocked by his attitude. Maybe he had money to waste on oil changes, but I wasn't going to waste money on something I could accomplish on my own.

I crawled back beneath the Jeep and loosened the drain plug with my socket wrench, letting a good amount of oil drain into the pan before tightening the plug back up. I didn't want to sabotage my vehicle to the point of a possible breakdown.

I heard footsteps and saw a pair of men's shoes standing in front of me.

"Did you have second thoughts about kissing me goodbye?" I yelled from beneath the Jeep.

The boy detective's face came into view as he squatted down and peered at me under the car. *Could this day get any worse*?

"There you go, flirting with me again," he chuckled.

"Detective Kendall," I sighed.

I scooched out from beneath the Jeep. Like the first time I'd met him, Jace Kendall's silhouette was blocking out the brilliant Colorado sun behind him, creating an angelic glow around him.

He extended his hand to help me up. After a brief deliberation, I took his hand, and he pulled me to my feet with ease. I offered him the rag from my pocket, and he wiped his hands. Opening his mouth as if to say something, he stopped.

"What?" I asked, annoyed.

"You have," he touched his cheek and then pointed to mine. Using the corner of the rag he wiped the smudge from my cheek.

"Thanks," I replied tentatively. "To what do I owe this unwelcomed visit, Detective Kendall?"

Kendall handed the dirty rag back to me and I wiped my hands the best I could. A foolish grin crossed the detective's lips.

"What?" I growled again, growing impatient with him.

"You change your own oil?"

"Uh, yeah. I suppose you're going to comment on how filthy I am too?" I added indicating my dirty clothes.

"Not at all. I just don't know many women of your…"

"Of what? My age?"

He laughed aloud, holding out his hands. "Why do you keep thinking that I'm implying you're old? You also did it when I helped you down the steps at the church when the pastor was killed."

"Because I *am* old, and I don't need to be reminded of it," I groaned.

"Ms. Windsor, you are not old."

"Well thank you very much, detective," I responded graciously as heat warmed my cheeks. I thought about declaring him my new best friend, as I usually did when someone said I didn't look as old as I was, but then I thought better of it. God knows I didn't need Jace Kendall thinking I was actually flirting with him, *that* was a headache I just didn't need.

As usual an awkward silence filled the space between us.

"Is there a reason you stopped by?" I asked him again.

He raised his index finger at me. "Yes, I know your penchant for seeing these crimes solved. I want you to assure me you're going to steer clear of this investigation, and let me and my colleagues handle this case once I get it reopened."

I opened my mouth but pursed my lips.

"I'll try," I conceded quickly.

"I need more than an 'I'll try'," he countered sternly, raising his eyebrows. "You've put yourself into dangerous positions twice now. Actually, more than twice."

I rolled my eyes and let out a sigh.

"Fine."

"Fine, what?"

"I will let you and your colleagues handle the case and not get involved," I told him with every intention of keeping my word to the boy child detective.

"I'm going to hold you to it," he declared, his finger still pointing in my direction while he backed away towards his blue sedan. Before getting into his vehicle, he gave me one last stern look.

I stood on the stoop of The Back Porch and watched him get into his car. Helen opened the door behind me as Kendall pointed at me once again.

“Who’s that?” She asked, nodding towards the car.

“That? That is the boy child detective, Jace Kendall.”

Helen slapped me on the shoulder. “You didn’t think to introduce him to me?”

“I was kinda busy getting my butt chewed, thank you very much,” I answered. “Who’s the cougar now wanting to be introduced?”

“Oooo, who’s that cute young thing?” Darla mewed as she walked up, peering into the blue sedan.

“Your sister’s hot young detective,” Helen responded, crossing her arms over her chest. “She didn’t feel the need to introduce us.”

“No wonder you want to be a cougar,” Darla grinned at me. “He’s gorgeous.”

“What was he doing here?” Helen asked.

"He came to make me promise to not immerse myself into his investigation this time," I replied staring at Kendall's taillights.

"So, you just drained the oil from your Jeep for nothing?" Helen continued.

"It would appear so," I muttered. "He probably has someone watching the place, so I'll never be able to take The Beast now."

Looking up and down the paved road, I tried to determine if there was anyone watching the place or an unmarked vehicle in sight. There was nothing on the street out of the ordinary, as far as I could tell.

"I'll bet mom's car needs an oil change," Darla chimed in, offering me another opportunity.

"I suppose I can't help it if I'm riding shotgun and you take the car to get the oil changed," I contended with a grin.

I popped into my parent's house, leaving Darla waiting in the car. Dad was on the couch with his extenda-ear thingy on his head. Lifting one side off of his ear, I told him I needed to borrow them for a couple of hours, and I'd bring them back asap.

"It's really important, dad," I assured him, nodding my head up and down frantically.

"How am I going to listen to this western?" He shouted angrily while pointing at the TV.

"The old-fashioned way," I told him, turning up the volume on the remote with the quick push of a button, then tossing it to him. "Love you."

"You dang girls, Darla taking your mother's car, so she has to use mine and now you're taking my headphones. Some things never change, just like when you girls were in high school," he grumbled, turning the volume up even higher on the television.

Kissing his cheek, I hurried out the door before he could protest any further and insist on my returning his headphones. Apparently, his hearing was way more impaired than I'd known, because I could hear 'the Duke' hollering at a bunch of young cowboys all the way out in the driveway.

"What did he say?" Darla asked with a grin.

"He complained about you taking mom's car and me stealing his headphones. Said it was just like when we were in high school, so I grabbed them, kissed his head, and ran."

"Is he watching The Cowboys with John Wayne?" Darla asked, craning her head towards the house.

Unable to contain myself, I sniggered like villain Dick Dastardly's dog, Muttley, from the Saturday morning cartoon, Wacky Racers, nodding my head up and down.

"I hope the neighbors don't call the cops about a shootout on St. Augustine Drive," Darla added.

I snorted, tears forming at the corners of my eyes. "I'd love to be here when mom gets back from the grocery store. I can hear her now, 'what the hell is going on in here? It sounds like Wyatt Earp and Doc Holiday at the OK Corral."

"It's exactly what she's going to say," Darla giggled, as she pounded on the steering wheel several times before putting the car in reverse and backing out of the driveway. The two of us giggled all the way to the mechanic's shop.

5

Darla pulled my mom's car into the middle bay of Big Al's mechanic's shop. Rolling the window down, my nostrils were overwhelmed with the scent of burnt oil. You know the smell when you spill oil on the engine, and it takes a while to burn off?

My eyes scanned the garage, and I couldn't help but notice the sign on the wall by each bay which read, 'Warning: Open floor, Watch your step'. On the sign was also a triangle with a stick figure falling backwards into the pit. I shuddered inwardly, thinking about the fall young Dax Rubins had taken within these very walls.

I hoped to be able to pick up any conversations on either side of us with my dad's bionic headphones. Unfortunately for me, Steve Austin's girlfriend, Jamie Sommers' version of the bionic ear was far superior to this generic thing I had pilfered from my father.

I glanced at my sister and noticed she was staring at me strangely.

"What?"

"Tell me more about these visions of dead people. Is it a 'Sixth Sense' thing like Bruce Willis had in the movie?"

"No. Did you even watch the movie?" I asked confused. "Bruce Willis wasn't seeing ghosts; the little boy was."

"Whatever," Darla wriggled her hands in the air with an exaggerated eyeroll. "Are you going to explain it or not?"

"I don't have visions of the victims, I see everything through their eyes, the way it happened at the time. It all started when I bought this adorable pair of pink cat-eye glasses. The lady who owned them was murdered in her bungalow at the nursing home where she was living. Until her murder was solved, every time I put them on, I would see the last several minutes of her life, including her death. In this case, it was the Eagle's t-shirt I was telling you about. The boy who wore it was murdered here in this garage. Someone pushed him backwards into one of the grease pits."

"That is freakishly weird, but also freakishly cool in a creepy kinda way. I don't think I'd like it if it happened to me, though," she frowned. "It would freak me out."

I shrugged. "I was able to help solve her murder and the murder of a local pastor because of buying their items which had been donated to thrift shops here in town. I want to help with this boy's murder too."

"It probably helps to bring closure to those families." She paused before adding, "and you get to practice your cougar moves on that young hottie of a detective."

I used the middle finger of my left hand to scratch my ear. Now ignoring her, I put my dad's headphones on and started listening. In my excitement, I had failed to realize these wouldn't help at all. They were programed to work with the device connected to my parent's television. (Scratch the earlier comment about my sister being brilliant.)

My poor father was at home blaring the TV for no reason at all. I vowed to pick up a chocolate milkshake or a banana spilt for him on my way home for his troubles.

"This isn't going to work," I began, pulling the headphones off. "They only work with the box that's connected to the TV."

"Didn't even think about that part. We'll both have to just listen then," Darla told me, craning her neck to the left towards the open driver's side window.

I did as she did, craning my neck towards the passenger side window. All either of us heard was the buzzing of tools, idling engines, and shouts from one employee to another.

Something odd occurred to me as I glanced around at the employees in the garage. They were all named Al of some sort. The shirts they wore sported the names Alan, Albert, Alvin, Alister and Alonso. I vowed to see if I could make out a name of the person who pushed Dax, the next time I put the t-shirt on. It also had me wondering what name was on Dax Rubin's shirt.

Several whirring clicks from my left drew my attention. My sister was slyly raising her phone and taking pictures of the employees inside the garage.

"Maybe something will come of these," she suggested pointing to her phone.

A booming voice shouted out, bringing all the other sounds within the garage to a halt. Darla turned her camera in his direction and continued to click away.

"I can't believe I actually pay all of you imbeciles for such incompetence. This is the third order you have screwed up," a large man shouted, his face beet red and shaking several papers in his beefy hand. 'Big Al' was embroidered over his left breast. "If this next shipment is messed up, I swear by everything that is holy, I'm going to … I have half a mind to fire the lot of you. Starting with you."

Big Al pointed to a young man with Albert on his shirt. Albert pointed to himself and mouthed 'me'?

"No, not you, you idiot. Her." Big Al pointed sternly to the young woman next to Albert. Her uniform read, Allison.

The young woman burst into tears and ran out one of the big bay doors, her hands covering her face.

"Hopefully, she won't come back," the big man yelled. "Now get back to work, all of you."

He disappeared back through the door from which he'd entered the garage area,

"I wonder what *that* was all about?" my sister asked, looking at me.

"Me too," I responded. "But it sounds like there are going to be some personnel changes here at Big Al's Automotive."

"Sounded a bit chauvinistic to me, only threatening to fire the girl," Darla huffed.

The oil in my mother's car was changed within thirty minutes and we were back out on the streets.

"Now what?" Darla asked.

"I don't know," I shrugged.

"Let's go to the drug store up the street and get some pictures printed," my sister suggested, looking giddy.

It felt like printing pictures of strangers without their permission was a violation of their privacy, but I had a murder to solve so I nodded in approval.

"Don't you think this guy has shifty eyes," Darla asked, pointing to an 8x10 of someone named Alvin.

I looked at the picture she held in her hand.

"Dax was killed over two years ago. I wonder how many of these people have been there since then?" I thought aloud as I set the rest of the pictures on the dashboard.

"Too bad we can't ask that hottie detective of yours," my sister added, wiggling her eyebrows.

"Would you please stop about Kendall being a hottie, you're old enough to be his mother. And he is not my detective," I complained loudly.

Darla scowled. "It doesn't mean I can't appreciate a good-looking guy when I see one. You don't think he's good looking?"

"Yes, I think he is a good-looking young man. Emphasis on young. Can we please get back to working on these pictures?" I suggested pointing to the pile.

Darla grabbed the stack of photos from the dashboard and shuffled through them.

After examining the prints and determining a couple of them were some shady looking characters, we decided we needed to do some further investigation. Scanning through the photos, I wondered if any of these guys were Trent Powers; the guy who was now engaged to Dax Ruben's old girlfriend, Prentiss.

Darla and I returned to Big Al's to scope it out. We were in luck. The two guys we were interested in were still inside working. The shop would be closing soon, so my sister and I waited in the parking lot of a cheap motel across the street from the garage.

The two young men exited the shop and stood near the street, the taller one pulled out a cigarette and lit it, flicking the match to the ground. After several minutes, a small red truck with an extended cab pulled up with a young woman driving.

If one of these guys was Trent, could this woman be Prentiss? The picture Kendall had shown me had been taken from behind them, so it only showed their backs and the backs of their heads. I had no way of truly knowing if any of these people were who I thought they could be.

The pair of mechanics piled into the vehicle; the one up front kissed the woman driving. Evidence was accumulating, leading me to believe this could be Trent and Prentiss.

Since Darla hadn't experienced 'tailing a subject' (are you picking up on the cop lingo), she insisted I drive. We each jumped out and ran around to each other's side of the car.

During my first 'case' (more cop lingo), I'd lost the woman I was following. Since then, I'd learned how to hang back just enough not to be seen but close enough not to lose the person I was tailing. I'd found myself practicing following cars while I'd driven around town lately.

The trio pulled into a liquor store on North Murray Blvd. The guy in the backseat went inside and came out carrying two six-packs of bottled beer. It was too dark to make out what brand they had a liking for.

The truck made its way to North Powers Blvd and then over to Tutt, where they continued north. About a quarter of a mile along Tutt, a beer bottle flew from the back passenger window and smashed onto the sidewalk in an explosion of shattering glass.

"What the hell is wrong with these people?" my sister protested, digging around in her purse, and pulling out an old receipt and pen. "I'm reporting them. Get closer so I can get their license plate number."

I sped up, allowing her to see the license plate.

Just before reaching Dublin Road, they cut off the lights and pulled over near a complex of townhomes. I passed slowly, my sister scribbling away on the tiny scrap of paper.

Pulling into the entrance of the townhomes, I cut my own lights and flipped a U. Luckily, there was a boxwood hedge lining the entrance which concealed my mother's car quite nicely.

From our vantage point, we watched the two men exit the truck and lower the tailgate. They proceeded to try to creep inconspicuously towards the townhomes, occasionally raising their fingers to their lips, but they stumbled forward in their efforts, clearly intoxicated.

Pausing momentarily at the closest patio to the street, the two men grabbed the handles of barbeque grill on the cement slab and started to run awkwardly, jostling the silver piece of equipment between them. Both men were jerked off their feet as the grill came to an abrupt halt and toppled over, as the grill came to the end of its chain tether.

My sister and I burst into maniacal hysteria as the two would-be thieves roiled in pain on the lawn, which was suddenly illuminated by the back patio lights of the townhome they attempted to burgle from.

Scrambling to their feet, the two Al's stumbled and crawled towards the truck, and jumped into the back. The driver gunned the engine and sped away, tires screeching. Back on the lawn a heavyset man in an open bathrobe and boxer shorts was standing on the lawn shaking his fist and thrusting his middle finger at the fleeing vehicle.

"We need to report this too," Darla choked out through her laughter.

"I can't. The boy child detective warned me to stay out of this investigation. It was freaking priceless though."

"Those two definitely possess criminal DNA," my sister proclaimed.

"I'm not so sure petty theft is tantamount to murder," I replied. "But still, you have to wonder."

"Maybe the dead guy knew they were stealing from the garage, and they found out, then offed him before he could tell anyone," she suggested. "I knew they were shady from their pictures."

The thought, 'you can't judge a book by its cover' popped into my head, maybe in this case you could.

"There was only one person there when he was pushed," I explained.

"Well, maybe that person drew the short straw and had to be the one to take him out while the other waited in the background."

I think her ADD was rubbing off on me because the strangest thought erupted from mouth. "Isn't it funny how 'take out' can be food, dating or killing someone?"

She paused for a moment. "And, if you're a praying mantis, it could be all three at once," she added.

Both of us cracked up at this remark. Once we caught our breath my sister looped back to what had just occurred.

"Did you see the way they were jerked back off their feet? That had to hurt," she shrieked.

My jaws were aching from the frivolity their mishap had inflicted.

"It's the most entertaining evening I've had in a long time," my sister declared.

"You don't get out much, do you?"

"You're a fine one to talk," she needled, giving me a side-eye glance.

"I'm actually seeing someone," I told her placing my fingertips on my sternum.

"Get out. Who?"

"A very nice gentleman named Artie. He recently moved here from the east coast."

"A gentleman? Ooooo, he sounds posh."

"You don't know the half of it. He was raised by his very eccentric aunt and went to boarding school. He speaks *very* properly," I mimicked, in my best British accent.

"So, what's he doing with you?" A quizzical look escaped her.

She was lucky I was in a good mood after witnessing those would-be thieves get theirs. Otherwise, I might have stopped the car and made her walk.

But I realized something and did pull the Jeep over to the side of the road.

"You're gonna make me walk, aren't you?" My sister asked, looking shocked.

"I thought about it, but no. Do you know who that was?" I asked, pointing back towards the townhomes.

She shook her head.

"Those guys tried to steal Big Al's barbeque grill. They were trying to steal from their boss."

"My idea doesn't sound so farfetched after all, now does it."

Not so farfetched, indeed.

The middle console vibrated as a call came in on my cellphone. Oh no, it was Artie's name that came up on the screen. I had completely forgotten he was going to pick me up for dinner.

"Aren't you going to answer it?"

"No, I'm driving."

"We're stopped," my sister pointed out.

I put the car into gear and pulled away from the curb.

In truth, I did *not* want to explain to Artie where I was and why I had stood him up, while my sister listened in. I also needed to figure out something to tell him without hurting his feelings because I'd forgotten him.

"You need to get a hands-free system." My nosy sister informed me and then picked up my phone before I could stop her. "Who's Artie?"

"Just a client." I snapped, reaching for my phone.

"Why would a client be calling you at this time of night?" She raised her eyebrows at me, pulling my phone out of reach. "Ohhhhhh, this is *the* guy. Look, he's left a voicemail."

Darla's fingertips moved nimbly on my phone. Through the speaker, I heard Artie's message.

"Marlie, this is Artie. It is after six o'clock. I stopped by earlier to pick you up for dinner, but you were not at your apartment. I drove past your shop and saw your car was still there, and all the lights were off. Are you having car trouble after changing your oil yourself?

I told you; you should have taken it to a shop. Please call me and let me know if you are alright. I'm worried. I can come pick you up if you need me to."

"He sounds sweet," Darla cooed. "He seems concerned with your welfare. You should call him back."

I made a mental note to call my son, Hub, and ask him how to lock my phone from snooping sisters.

"Aren't you going to call him back?" She asked eagerly, offering me my phone back.

"I will when I get home. First, I have to pick up 'the Beast' from the shop and then get rid of *you*."

"Ruude," my sister hissed.

After picking up my car and sending Darla on her way, I called Artie back. He picked up on the first ring.

"Marlie, are you alright? I have been so worried. Do you need me to come and get you from somewhere?"

"Artie, thanks, I'm fine. I was with my sister who's visiting from out of town, and I lost track of time.

I am so sorry. I'm really sorry you drove all the way to the apartment, and I wasn't there."

"It's fine, now that I know you are safe and not stranded somewhere or in any danger. I am breathing much easier."

He let out an audible sigh. "You didn't tell me your sister was coming into town."

"She surprised us yesterday, then showed up at the shop today, we just got carried away and lost track of time."

"I am just relieved you are alright. We can plan to do dinner another evening."

"Thank you for understanding, Artie. She lives in Nashville, and I don't get to see her very often."

"Well, I am pleased you were able to spend time with your sister then. I will come by The Back Porch and reschedule dinner with you for later this week. Sleep well, Darling."

"Thank you. Have a good night," I told him as I hung up.

I stared at my phone. Darling? Artie had never called me Darling before, it had taken him long enough to call me by my name, let alone, Darling. I found it vaguely disconcerting.

I was accosted by my nosy neighbor living in 211 (whom I referred to as W-cubed (Wicked Witch of the West), when I was walking to my apartment. She informed me that Artie had been there, knocking on my door and peeking in through my front window.

"A smartly dressed gentleman was here looking for you," she informed me. "Your yappy little mutt would not stop barking until he walked away."

"That's my vicious little watch dog," I smiled.

Her face contorted into a mock smile, causing her eyes to nearly close with the exaggeration. "Watch dog, humph," she mocked, entering her own apartment, slamming the door behind her.

I stuck my tongue out at her closed door, childish I know but that woman brought out the worst in most people. “Hateful, old witch,” I muttered, pulling out my keys.

My ‘yappy little mutt’ greeted me when I opened the door.

“You just ignore that wicked old witch,” I told him, picking him up and rubbing his head.

6

An annoying buzzing from my nightstand, woke me from a pleasant dream I was enjoying, involving my man, Don.

"This better be good," I grumbled into the phone, not caring who was on the other end of the line.

"And a good morning to you too," I heard a voice sarcastically reply from the other end of the conversation. "Sounds like someone woke up on the wrong side of the bed."

Being half asleep, the only thing that registered was it was a male voice on the other end. I looked at the name on the screen of my cell phone: Boy Child Detective.

"Is there something I can help you with at this early hour, detective?"

"I don't think most people call ten o'clock early, but you *are* different. I'll give you that."

I shot up and looked out my window, the sky was a dull gray.

“Is it storming out? It’s so dark.”

“It did snow a couple of inches overnight, but there’s a solar eclipse going on,” he informed me.

Throwing the covers off and bounding to the window, I peered outside. The eclipse was creating a spectacular pattern on the ground beneath the trees. A phenomenon I had been hoping to photograph.

“Dang, I’m missing it. Why are you calling, detective?”

“I was wondering if you had any more information for me from the t-shirt.”

“No,” I replied honestly. “My sister is in town. And her and I were out and about yesterday so I didn’t get the chance.”

“You have a sister? Maybe she’ll want to ask me out too.”

Darla’s comments about Kendall being a hottie coursed through my thoughts.

"Oh my gawd… I don't… want to go out… with you," I insisted, cradling the phone between my shoulder and ear as I began changing out of my pajama top and shorts.

"How could you say something so hurtful," He whined, then added, "What are you doing?"

"What do you mean what am I doing?"

"You sound as if you're wrestling with someone," he implied.

Before I could think better of it, I responded with, "I'm trying to get dressed so I can get outside to take some pictures during the eclipse."

"Oh… you don't have any clothes on?"

I could feel the dreaded smirk all the way from downtown.

"I'm hanging up now," I told him and pushed the red button on my screen.

Throwing the phone onto the bed, I dressed quickly and was putting my shoes on when the phone buzzed again. I didn't even say hello when he called back.

"What?"

"You're quite the morgenmuffel," he informed me.

"A morgan what?"

"Morgenmuffel. It's German for a person who's grumpy in the mornings and doesn't like to wake up early."

"That is the most idiotic thing I've heard in a while," I snapped.

"You *did* get up on the wrong side of the bed," he repeated.

"Yes, I did. I forgot to set my alarm and now I'm running behind."

"Well, then you should be thanking me for calling and waking you up, instead of grumbling at me," Kendall stated.

Had he not awakened me from such a pleasant dream, I may have sincerely thanked him. He was correct, I should thank him, but he was soooo iritating.

"Thank you, detective," I cooed sweetly into the phone.

"Do I hear a note of sarcasm in that statement?"

"A note? No, more like a damn symphony, I'd say."

"I think you need to go back to bed. Do you want me to come tuck you in?" He asked in a seductive tone.

I hung up on the detective for the second time this morning. He must have gotten the message because he didn't call back a third time.

The images I captured were even more spectacular upon the layer of fresh snow covering the ground.

After clicking off several more pictures of the stunning patterns from the solar eclipse, I went back upstairs and let Peyton out, who rushed to do his business since I'd forgotten to set my alarm. I was surprised he hadn't tried to rouse me. I'd have to search the apartment in case he had left me his own surprise.

Phoning Helen, I explained I'd forgotten to set my alarm and I'd be there within the next forty-five minutes.

"Don't rush, it's been pretty slow this morning," she told me. "But you can bring something sweet and tasty when you come in."

When I arrived, two of my favorite patrons were inside browsing. A couple of older ladies who'd become pretty regular customers, JoAnne and Lisa, were so much fun to listen to as they bantered back and forth between them. Plus, they'd helped me win a bet with Helen and earned me a Mexican dinner and margaritas, so they held a special place in my heart, if not my stomach and liver.

"We weren't sure if we'd see you today," Lisa smiled at me, as I hustled in and dumped my belongings on my desk and depositing a lavender bag on Helen's desk.

"I'm just running a little behind today," I explained.

Helen was showing JoAnne a tray of vintage jewelry, which the white-haired lady was oohing and aahing over.

"Will you hang on to this piece for me?" JoAnne asked my business partner. "I'm going to slip off to the ladies room."

"She has a bladder the size of a peanut," Lisa apprised me, in a rather loud whisper. "She knows the location of every toilet in the state."

Helen and I smiled, suppressing giggles.

A few moments later, JoAnne returned, a look of awe on her sweet face.

"I've never seen lilac scented hair spray before," JoAnne beamed, lightly bouncing her snowy locks.

Helen and I looked in astonishment at one another, our eyes growing wide. We didn't have any lilac scented hairspray in the restroom, only lilac scented air freshener.

Lisa looked at her companion in utter disbelief, her mouth open wide. Shaking her head, she walked to the back and returned in a moment with the can of lilac air freshener in her hand.

"This is air freshener, you goof. I keep telling you that you need new glasses," Lisa chastised her friend.

JoAnne gave her a sneer and squinted at the can. “Hmm, I thought it said hair freshener. Assumed it was some newfangled product. It works great as hair spray and smells divine. Maybe I should write the company and share my idea.”

Placing her hand over her eyes, Lisa shook her head. “How have I stayed friends with you all these years?”

It took every ounce of restraint I had, not to burst into a fit of laughter. Looking over at Helen, I saw her struggling to maintain her composure as well.

After the ‘hair freshener’ incident, the two ladies browsed the shop some more, bickering with one another as they did. A little bit later, JoAnne stepped to the side with Helen to pay for the pieces of jewelry she’d chosen from the display case. Lisa stayed near me, chatting about the weather and other topics while she waited on her friend.

“You should come play Bingo with us some evening,” she was saying as JoAnne walked over to us. “We could use some young blood in the bingo hall.”

"I'd think that Marlie has better things to do than hang out playing bingo with the likes of us," JoAnne muttered, beginning to rummage around inside her cavernous purse.

"What are you looking for?" Lisa asked her snippily.

"My keys," JoAnne replied, continuing to search her bag.

"I drove," Lisa told her, jangling her own keys in front of JoAnne.

"Oh yeah," her friend smiled cheerfully, putting her purse on her shoulder, and heading for the door.

Helen walked them to the door and out to their car. She returned shaking her head with an enormous smile on her lips.

"Can you believe she used our air freshener as hairspray? I almost died," my business partner chortled.

"Not hair spray," I corrected, "hair freshener. Those two make my day every time they come in. I hope you and I are as entertaining as they are when we reach their age."

"I'd say 'their age' is creeping up on us faster than we'd like," she proposed.

Frowning, I nodded in agreement.

After our guests had departed, I relayed to Helen the happenings from the previous night's escapades with my sister and the would-be burglars.

"I wish I'd been there to see that," she confessed with a huge smile.

"It was extremely entertaining," I confirmed.

Later in the afternoon, with Helen's assistance, I was able to find an address for a Trent Powers, on the west side of Colorado Springs.

I left a little early and headed to the address which Helen had supplied, keeping my fingers crossed that this was indeed the Trent Powers I was looking for.

It was one of the older homes in Old Colorado City. This was going to prove to be difficult. The garage for the house was in the back down the alley and there were numerous cars on the street out front, though none directly in front of the house I was watching. I parked on the street, a few doors down, dug my binos out of the glove compartment and waited.

I'd like to say I waited patiently, but patiently is not a word I ascribe to, not for the long haul anyway. After about fifteen minutes, my eyes began to wander and focused in on the mountains as the sun began to sink down behind them.

The sunset was spectacular with its vast array of pink and orange hues mixed together in an artistic display in the sky above the shadowed, snow-covered mountains.

There is absolutely nothing quite as beautiful or more majestic than the sun setting behind the Colorado Rockies. It took my breath away every time I watched the sun go down over the ridge. I suppose living in such a beautiful city made me a bit biased.

The sound of a car door slamming shut brought me back to what I was here for: surveillance. Up the street a small gray car had pulled up in front of the house. At this distance in the dark, I was unable to determine the make and model.

A man got out of the driver's side and went around to the passenger door, opening it, he assisted a very pregnant young lady, who I assumed to be Prentiss Reeves. Taking her by the elbow, he helped her out of the vehicle and into the house.

Neither of these two individuals were part of the shenanigans which had taken place the previous evening.

Once the woman was inside, the man quickly returned to the vehicle and removed a child from the backseat. Through the binoculars, it appeared the child was sleeping. He gently carried the sleeping tot into the house and closed the door. Within moments, the porch light was switched on, illuminating the front of the home in a peaceful, evening splendor.

Now what, I thought as I sat there in the cold, pondering what to do next. There was nothing to do except come back tomorrow, early, to continue my surveillance.

I stopped at my parents' house and had dinner with them and Darla. Mom had made her famous green chili meat loaf with mashed potatoes and sautéed green beans in garlic butter. It was a feast fit for a king… or a very hungry vintage boutique owner, in my case.

7

When my alarm went off at 5:30 a.m., I had the brief desire to reset it for 8:00 and go back to sleep. But the vintage concert t-shirt hanging over the back of the chair in my bedroom urged me to get up and get cracking on solving this. And I didn't want to be a morgenfluffel, or whatever it was Kendall had referred to me as the day before.

Normally, my bedroom would be drenched in complete darkness at this hour of the morning, but I had failed to close the curtains last night, so the streetlamp outside my window glared violently into my sleeping quarters. Its yellowish glow illuminated the piece of clothing which was now the object of my most recent torment.

Not knowing what time Trent and Prentiss would be leaving, I wanted to make sure I was there when they started moving. I had spent an extraordinary amount of time away from the shop, trying to solve Rose O'Brien's murder and I didn't want to put Helen through it once more.

I popped through one of the drive-through coffee shops, ordering my signature white chocolate mocha and chocolate croissant. What better way to start my early morning surveillance? Helen would be proud. Now, let's not go down the healthy road. Forcing down some tasteless protein concoction was not my idea of a pick me up, especially at this hour.

The need for an early arrival had not been necessary. The first sign of life from inside the residence didn't occur until 10:30, when the front porch light was turned off.

About forty-five minutes later, the man whom I was assuming to be Trent Powers, walked a small boy to the car and secured him into the car seat, giving the child a kiss on the head before closing the car door.

Prentiss, or who I hoped was Prentiss, followed slowly, waddling down the front walkway and struggling to get in behind the steering wheel. Rolling down the window, she kissed the man on the lips and started the car.

I followed the car up I-25 to the North Academy Boulevard exit then over to Chapel Hills Mall, parking an aisle over from her car.

She struggled again to extricate herself from the small vehicle's confines. Her pregnancy was creating difficulties as she pulled the child from the back seat.

The squirming toddler freed himself from his mother's grasp and began running towards the mall entrance as fast as his little feet could carry him.

"Dax, stop! Get back here," she screamed out in panic.

Sprinting in the child's direction, I grabbed his hand, bringing his escape to a quick halt. He struggled against my hold and began wailing loudly for his mother, when he realized a stranger had a hold on him.

Prentiss made her way over to us and grabbed the child's other hand.

"Thank you," she panted, trying to catch her breath.

"You're welcome," I replied, releasing my grip on the rambunctious toddler.

"Dax, you can't run off like that," she scolded. "You could have been hit by a car."

"Play," he piped back, no longer screaming and wrestling against his mother's hold once more.

"Yes, we're going to go play, but not for too long. I have to find a gift for daddy's birthday and then get back home."

She directed another thank you and smile towards me as she ushered the anxious child into the mall.

She had called the child, Dax. I was sure now this was indeed Prentiss Reeves. Waiting for a moment, I followed at a slower pace, not wanting to arouse any suspicion she was being trailed.

Once inside, Prentiss entered the sporting goods store, made a quick purchase of some running shoes, and then headed straight for the play area, being dragged along by the child. Little Dax pulled from her grasp again and ran to the plastic structures which enticed children to play. At least there was no chance of the little boy being run over inside the mall.

I made my way up the staircase and watched from above, while the child played, and the mother got a short reprise. Knowing they'd be there for at least a bit; I did laps around the rectangular railing above the play area.

Helen and I had been imbibing in way too many sweets lately, so I took advantage of my time, trying to get in as many steps as I could before I had to get back into the car.

Thirty minutes later and sensing mom was about ready to leave, I hurried down the steps and casually approached Prentiss.

"He looks like he's having a fun time," I commented, watching the child scramble about the play area with abandon.

"He loves climbing on the playhouse," she replied. "Dax, we need to leave soon to go pick up daddy."

The boy made a pouty face but continued to enjoy his last few minutes of play.

"Dax. Such a unique name," I pried. "Is he named after his father?"

"He's named after his biological father," she volunteered, "but he died before Dax was born."

"I'm so sorry," I told her with all sincerity.

"After the funeral, I started dating his best friend and now we're engaged and have our own little one on the way," she pointed, indicating her round belly. "Dax, get down from there!"

Her shout caught the child off guard. He fell backwards off the plastic tree he'd been trying to scale, his head slamming into the soft flooring.

Talk about déjà vu. In my mind's eye, I relived the elder Dax's deathly plummet. Waves of anxiety attacked every nerve in my body.

Prentiss rushed to his side, clearly in a panic.

"Oh my goodness, you scared Mommy half to death," she trembled, scooping up the child and cuddling him tightly, tears streaming down her cheeks.

"Is he alright?"

"Yes, I think it frightened me more than it did him. His biological father died from a fall backwards and hitting his head on a concrete floor."

"No wonder you were so anxious," I empathized. If she'd only known that daddy Dax had been murdered, she may not have been so frightened.

"Dax and Trent, my fiancé, had a disagreement before the accident. We were afraid the cops might think Trent had pushed him after their argument and fist fight."

I just let her keep talking, if she was going to be what I liked to refer to as, an over-sharer, then so be it.

"Dax wasn't happy when he found out I was pregnant with this one," she rubbed the child's head. "He wanted to get out of the mechanics shop where he worked and make something of himself, not be strapped down with a wife and kid. He had aspirations of playing in the NFL and was hoping to play college ball with the Buffs up in Boulder. Trent was mad at him for his reaction and confronted him. They fought about it, and Trent left with a black eye and swollen lip. We all heard the next morning that Dax had fallen into the grease pit at work and died."

Letting go of the boy, he ran back and began climbing the structures once more, completely over his recent fall.

"Did the cops ever question your fiancé about the fight?"

"No," she replied in a hushed tone, shaking her head slightly, "they didn't ask, so I told Trent to keep quiet about it. I didn't want him to get into any trouble. But then they determined Dax had slipped and fallen on his own, so we just let it go."

"I see," was all I could think of to say.

"Dax, let's go get daddy. He has a surprise for you," his mother coaxed.

The child ran over to Prentiss, and she took him by the hand. She began gathering up her things the best she could, while still holding onto Dax Rubin's namesake. Offering to help, I carried her bags for her and walked back to the car with her where she loaded the boy into his car seat and thanked me for all my assistance. Wishing her luck, I watched her drive away.

I knew the boy child detective wasn't going to be happy with me following Prentiss, but this was information I'm sure he needed. Maybe it would be enough to have Dax's death looked into more closely. At least I hoped it would.

8

Driving the speed limit and taking as many side streets as I could, I took my time getting to Kendall's office, not relishing the lecture I was certain would accompany my sharing this information with him. How many times had he told me not to interfere? Too many for me to count. Subconsciously, I shifted in my set, preparing for the ass-chewing I knew would ensue once I arrived.

All the way downtown, I kept trying to think of ways to break it to him, without him blowing a gasket. I tried going through different conversations in my head. Somehow, they all ended up with him steaming mad and threatening once again to lock me up. Steeling myself for the worst, I knocked on his office door, and peered in.

His face brightened when he saw me, which was highly disconcerting, considering our past experiences, most of the time he would complain when I walked into his office. He jumped up and offered me a seat, something he'd never ever done before. I was beginning to wonder if I was in the right place and did a double take to make sure I was, indeed, in the correct office.

"Usually you aren't this happy to see me," I started.

"Are you here to tell me you discovered something new from the t-shirt?" He asked hopefully, sitting back down in his own chair.

"Not exactly," I said, looking up to avoid eye contact, then slowly turning my gaze back to him.

"What do you mean 'not exactly'," he asked sternly, tapping his fingers on his desk while his eyes zeroed in on me.

"I *do* have information for you, but I didn't get it from putting the shirt on again."

"How did you obtain the information you're about to share with me?" He asked, his jaw jutting forward.

"Does it really matter how I came by the information? Shouldn't it just matter that I *have* the information?"

"I'm not going to like the answer, am I?"

"Probably not," I replied, shaking my head.

He stared at me, his anger growing exponentially, as I watched his shoulders tighten and his back stiffen.

"Do you want it or not?"

"Is it pertinent to the case?"

"Possibly," I answered giving him a sideway glance.

"Tell me what you know," he demanded through narrowed eyes, "now!"

I jumped slightly in my seat.

"If you're going to be like that then I won't tell you what I found out," I dared aloud.

"You would withhold evidence in a murder case?" He asked forcefully.

"Well, only you, me and the killer know it was murder. As far as everyone else is concerned, it was an accident."

Kendall glared at me, his eyes burning into my consciousness, making me increasingly more and more uncomfortable.

"Alright, alright, but you should be more grateful and stop treating me as if *I* were the criminal here," I pouted.

The muscles in his neck strained as I told him about staking out Trent and Prentiss's house. He began grinding his teeth when I told him about subsequently following her to the mall and the conversation which had followed about Dax and Trent's altercation, Prentiss's pregnancy and Dax being the father who didn't want to be strapped down.

"Those little bastards lied to me," he stammered, slamming his fist on his desk.

I breathed a sigh of relief, at least his anger was focused on them now, instead of on me and my indiscretions.

"It explains why his knuckles were swollen and bruised. The medical examiner determined it was from hitting the wall when he fell through the floor. This gives me a motive for murder, for not one, but two people. Prentiss could have pushed him, or Trent could have done it, for that matter. A woman scorned is one of the oldest motives in time. Jealous lover? Happens every day."

I could see the wheels turning, so I kept mum, not wanting to draw any further attention to the fact I'd ignored his demands to stay out of his investigation. I stood slowly and slyly made my way to the door.

"Oh, and something else. Two of the guys who work at Big Al's tried to steal a barbeque grill the other night from a townhouse over off of Tutt, belonging to none other than Big Al himself," my words came out in a rush so I could high tail it out of there.

He gritted his teeth, and I could see the vein on his left temple pulsing. I decided to make my escape before he could make good on his threat of arresting me.

"Don't you even think about moving," he stammered through his clenched jaw, slamming his fist down hard on his desk.

I stopped in my tracks, contemplating how far my short legs would carry me before he caught up to me. *Not worth the pain*, I told myself.

"Get back in here and sit down," he commanded in a gruff voice.

I really didn't care for the tone he was using with me, but I conceded he did have cause. I'd promised not to involve myself in his investigation and hadn't done a very good job of keeping my word.

Slowly, I backed into his office and took the seat across from him, my hands in my lap.

"*What* is it going to take for me to get through to you?"

He was standing now, leaning across his desk and shouting.

I opened my mouth to speak but he continued on, covering my mouth with my hand, I sat stone still.

"Am I going to have to lock you up? So far, the threat of which has yet to deter you. Please, jump in here and give me some suggestions," he yelled, throwing his hands up.

I swallowed hard, not daring to move or speak. He began chewing me out again without waiting for my answer.

"So, not only did you stake out and follow Prentiss Reeves, but you followed two of the guys from the shop even after we'd had our discussion?

"One thing I hate more than someone lying to me, is a liar who thinks I'm stupid."

"I don't think you're stupid, Kendall…"

"There," he exclaimed, pointing an accusatory finger at me, "you admit you lied to me."

"I didn't lie on purpose," I explained, feeling the heat in my cheeks. "I just get to thinking about the cases and I can't help myself from wanting to resolve them. I'm only trying to help, Kendall," I grumbled, agitation rising in my voice.

He drew in a breath and blew it out slowly. “I know you’re only trying to help,” he stated more calmly, “but if the evidence we get is not obtained properly, then I can’t use it on the case. How can I bring Trent and Prentiss in after you followed her? What could I possibly say to warrant them being brought in for questioning, especially since it was never ruled a homicide? I can’t just say a little birdie told me Dax was murdered and the two of you failed to disclose the argument which preceded his demise.”

He stared at me with questioning eyes.

I didn’t have an answer for him. I didn’t have a law degree to understand all the intricacies of our justice system. If only Victoria McNasty could find it in her evil soul to believe me, then we could ask her. But no, she was Satan’s sister and changing her mind would take an act from the Almighty above.

9

I stared at the shirt hanging over the back of the chair, knowing after this was solved, if it *was* ever solved, I'd never be able to use it to sleep in. Nope, this rare treasure would have to go to the shop in hopes another Eagles groupie would purchase it for themselves.

But for now… I walked to the chair, dreading each step.

"I have to be missing something," I berated myself, anger stirring within me. Taking a deep breath and letting it out slowly, I picked the shirt up once more.

"Concentrate," I told myself as I clenched it tight in my fist. Slipping my arms in and then over my head, I let the vision come. But nothing happened, not one damn thing. I took the shirt off and stared at it.

"You've got to be kidding me," I uttered in disbelief, throwing my head back and rolling my eyes.

I took off the shirt I'd been wearing and put the vintage t-shirt over my head and slipped my arms through the sleeves one more time.

Darkness obscured everything in the garage. There was only a minimal amount of light coming in from the streetlights outside.

The pain in my knuckles burned, irritating me. This time I felt Dax Rubin's anger, though I wasn't entirely certain who it was directed at: Prentiss, Trent or possibly someone else? Knowing what I knew about Prentiss' pregnancy and his altercation with Trent, it could be one of them, but then the raspy voice came from the darkness,

"I warned you, you're either with me or you'll suffer the consequences."

I strained to try to make out the person coming towards me in the dark, trying to see what they were wearing or to make out any other useful information. The only thing I was able to note was whoever was approaching through the darkness was roughly the same height and build as Dax Rubins. Inhaling in, I could only smell stale oil and burned rubber.

"I told you; I'm not getting involved with you."

"And I told *you*, you don't have a choice. I always get what I want."

The figure took another step towards me. Stepping back, I was at the edge of the grease pit, my attention riveted on not falling, and then came the push. Panic ensued as my arms windmilled about trying to keep from going over the edge, but it was no use. I fell backwards through the hole in the floor, landing with a resounding thud through my head.

As the blackness flooded in on me, the last thing I saw was the figure standing above, looking down on my dying body.

A wetness on my cheek brought me around. I was lying on the floor; Peyton sat next to me and licked my cheek again.

I sat up. Ripping the shirt off, I threw it across the room as far as I could.

"I can't do this anymore," I screamed, feeling defeated and depressed. "I just can't."

Peyton jumped at my outburst and hightailed it down the hall. My poor little dog thought I was screaming at him.

Sitting on the bed, I threw myself backwards and stared at the ceiling.

"Why is this happening to me?" I shouted, the tears coming in a torrent.

Maybe my sister was right, and I should stop buying old used crap, then I wouldn't have to deal with these visions of people's deaths any longer.

Grabbing my phone from the bedside table, I pushed the screen for Helen's number through blurry eyes. After two rings she answered.

"I can't do this anymore," I cried. "I'm lying here half naked and screaming. Poor Peyton thinks I'm yelling at him. I'm done."

"Marlie?" came the voice through the phone, but it wasn't Helen's voice. I looked at the screen. I had mistakenly called the boy child detective and *not* my best friend.

Damnit, did I just tell Jace Kendall I was half naked? Just shoot me…

I jammed my finger down on the red end call button and let out a half scream, half breath. I felt as if the room were closing in on me.

In my mind's eye, I could picture Kendall sitting at home, staring at his cell phone and bursting into uncontrollable fits of laughter at what I'd just relayed.

My phone rang. Boy Child Detective came up as the caller Id. I stuffed the phone under my pillow until it stopped ringing. Next came the text.

'Answer the phone. I know you're there.'

The cellphone rang again a minute or so later.

"Stop laughing at me," I demanded as I touched the screen, my voice shaking through my tears.

"I'm not laughing. I know this has to take a toll on you reliving the deaths of these people."

The tears came with a vengeance now, and I couldn't trust myself to speak. I sat there sobbing into the phone while Kendall patiently waited for me to calm down to the point I was able to at least utter something coherent.

"I feel useless on this. I haven't been able to tell you anything new from the t-shirt. And I just can't relive that boy's death over and over," I bawled.

"You're doing fine. You were able to confirm for me that Dax was indeed murdered. Which is something I didn't know for certain until you came to my office. And though I don't *condone* it, you brought me valuable information about Trent and Dax's altercation before he died. I can also look into the two guys and woman who tried to pilfer Big Al's barbeque."

His words brought me some comfort but not enough to stem my tears.

"Would you like me to come over?" He asked calmly.

"No," I shouted into the phone. It was the last thing I needed; having Jace Kendall show up at my apartment to comfort me.

"Is there anything I can do for you?"

"Yes, solve this case so I can live in peace," I blubbered at him.

"I'll do what I can," he pledged. "And Marlie…"

"Yes," I sniffled.

"Put some clothes on."

I began crying all over again and hung up. Now I was sure he was laughing at his house. I had made an utter and complete fool of myself by misdialing Helen's number.

When I finally composed myself, I called Helen, making sure it was her this time.

"I just made the biggest fool of myself," I bellowed into the phone. "I thought I had dialed you, but I called Kendall and told him I was lying half naked and screaming at my dog."

"Why are you half naked and why are you screaming at Peyton?"

"I put the shirt on to try to see the vision again, but it didn't work until I took my regular shirt off. I guess the damn thing has to be touching my skin to work."

"Okay, you still didn't tell me why you are half naked?" She prodded.

"When the vision was over, I peeled off the shirt and threw it across the room. I was so upset I tried to call you but called *him* instead."

"Freud would tell you, *you* actually meant to call Kendall because of your underlying feelings for him."

"Whose side are you on anyway?" I screamed.

"Are you yelling at me?"

"Yes."

"I'm just trying to help you deal with these feelings you have for the hot young detective. You don't need to shout at me."

"You have been absolutely no help."

"You're not crying anymore," she pointed out.

"I hate you."

"You love me, and you know it."

"Good night," I growled into the phone.

"Good night. I'll see you in the morning."

Dropping the phone on the bed next to me, I laid there questioning my own sanity.

Did I have underlying feelings for the boy child detective?

10

Helen's black Chevy Avalanche was already in the parking lot when I arrived at the shop. I groaned inwardly. I'd slept like crap and was in no mood for her ridicule or psychobabble. But, to my surprise she was on her best behavior this morning.

"Did you get any sleep?" She asked, concern apparent in her voice.

"Barely," I confessed through my blurry eyes. My face felt as if the bags under my eyes were touching my chin. I felt so lousy I hadn't even looked in the mirror this morning or put any makeup on.

"Sit down, I'll be right back," she ordered.

Following her instructions, I sat and waited.

She returned several minutes later with a cool wet cloth and a steaming mug.

"Drink this and put this over your eyes," she directed, handing me the cup and putting the cloth on my desk.

I blew across the top of the rim, sending steam billowing away from me and took a sip. My throat burned as I swallowed, not from the heat but from whatever she'd put into my tea.

"Are you trying to poison me?" I choked out.

"I put some whiskey in your tea, just drink it."

Doing as I was told, I downed the tea, then leaned back and put the cool towel over my eyes. I sat there for about fifteen minutes, letting the coolness soothe my weary eyes.

Tossing the cloth on my desk, I leaned forward, placing my elbows on my knees and my hands over my face. I stared at the floor through my fingers and shook my head.

"I can't believe I called Kendall last night."

"I…"

My hand shot out with a finger pointing at my business partner. "Don't even!"

Even with my eyes glued to the floor, I could feel her smile. "I'm sorry I've been giving you such a hard time about having a thing for the detective and being a cougar."

"I know you're just teasing me," I mumbled to the floor, "but it's starting to get old."

I felt her hand on my back. "You know I would do just about anything for you."

Glancing up, I eyed her suspiciously. "Just about anything? There are limits for what you'd do for me?"

She beamed. Her smile was contagious, and I felt the tension in my body melt away as I began to giggle.

We spent the rest of the morning dusting shelves and redoing displays, setting up new vignettes to showcase specific pieces.

Around noon, I placed an order with the deli around the corner. "What do you want on your Italian sub?" I asked Helen.

"Lettuce, tomato, pepperoncinis, salt, pepper, vinegar and oil," she responded from behind a shelf.

"Oil. I forgot about my oil," I said into the receiver.

"Excuse me?" the deli worker on the other end asked.

"I'm sorry, I was talking to myself. How soon will our order be ready?"

"We should have it over to you in about twenty minutes."

"Thank you," I told her and hung up the phone.

I bit my lower lip and glanced at my business partner. "I never replaced the oil in the Jeep. I need to get it taken care of."

"Why not take it over to Big Al's and see if you can discover anything new. What's he gonna do? Arrest you?" She cackled.

"He does keep threatening to do just that."

"I think you'd like it if he put you in handcuffs." Her offhand comment caught me off guard.

"You're starting this again?"

"Sure, why not?" She gave me a blasé faire shrug and continued typing on her keyboard.

I considered strangling her but then I'd have to explain it all to her husband, Mike. I was pretty sure I could claim it was a crime of passion and use him as a character witness at my trial. But the image of Kendall putting me into the handcuffs, which Helen had mentioned, drove the thought from my mind in expedited fashion.

Once we'd finished lunch, my irritating business partner kept prodding me to get my butt down to the garage before it closed. "All I need is for that white monster of yours to die. Then I'll be toting you around town, looking for a new car for who knows how long."

"Gee, thanks."

She pointed towards the front door. "Go."

I packed up my belongings, loaded them into the Jeep and headed towards Big Al's.

Pulling 'the beast' into the bay I was directed to, I requested an oil change and sat patiently, windows down, while I waited, telling myself I wasn't doing anything wrong because I really did need to get my oil taken care of. Didn't I? Somehow, I didn't find myself very convincing.

"Big Al, ain't gonna be happy if another shipment is messed up again," one of the Al's told the other in a lull in the noise.

Shipment? I wondered if they could possibly be talking about a drug shipment. But we were in a mechanic's shop, so a shipment could be nothing more than what it was supposed to be, auto parts. None the less, I felt the need to mention it to Kendall, consequences be damned.

I knew for certain he'd be livid if I hadn't kept my word again, but he wouldn't have this information, if I had kept it. Plus, he'd been very understanding by the time I left his office the other day, so maybe….

The car next to me, done with their oil change, pulled out through the back bay exit. Underneath, I saw something hanging down. It appeared to be a plastic bag filled with a white substance. It wasn't hanging down far enough to reach the pavement, but there was definitely something there. Because of the angle, I was unable to make out the full plate number on the brown Toyota exiting in front of me, but this was information I knew would benefit the boy child detective with his investigation.

Opening my phone, I added a note with all the names of the employees I observed working, to better help the police. I needed to get down to CSPD with this information and share it with Kendall.

As I pulled out onto Platte, I saw a flashing light behind me. There was no mistaking the familiar blue unmarked sedan.

"What do you think you're doing?" He barked, as I rolled the window down. "I knew you couldn't, or wouldn't, keep your word to me about immersing yourself in this investigation. Which is why I was across the street, on my day off none the less, to make sure you stayed away from this, but no, here you are, once again."

"I needed my oil changed," I snapped back. "I …"

"Bull, you just changed it yourself a few days ago. Remember, I was there," Kendall interrupted.

"I must have done something wrong. My oil light keeps coming on," I argued.

"And you just happened to take it to the shop where I'm working a cold case, in which you found the t-shirt of the victim and relived his murder? Right."

"What makes you think I don't always bring my car here?"

He tapped the little sticker in the upper left corner of the windshield placed there from my last visit to The Oil King over two years ago and cocked his head.

"I don't need you interfering in any pending investigation."

"Hmm, I think I've heard *that* somewhere before," I mocked, scratching my head with my middle finger.

"I mean it, Marlie. I'll arrest you this time," he growled through the open window.

"Ha, you can't keep me from getting my oil changed at the location of my choosing. And since when do you call me, Marlie?"

"I figured since I've had to save your ass twice now, we should be on a first name basis."

"Duncan saved my ass the last time. You were late to that party."

"The point is *you*, as a civilian, have placed yourself in harm's way twice by being where you shouldn't have been. So, if I have to lock you up to keep you safe then I'll do it."

"Need I remind you those cases wouldn't have been solved if I hadn't interfered."

"Damnit, Marlie."

"I'm not a child, quit treating me like one."

"Then stop acting like one."

"You don't understand," I quaked, my shoulders convulsing.

"I don't understand what?" He asked harshly.

"Once I have these visions, they become part of me. It's like the dead have chosen me to speak for them. I have to help solve these cases. They haunt me."

My hands were gripping the steering wheel, turning my knuckles white. By now tears were running down my cheeks.

"Spare me those big alligator tears. I'm not falling for it."

My left hand popped up with true intent this time; middle finger extended. "Bite me, Kendall," I yelled back through my tears. "You are a major, A-hole."

I turned the key in the ignition, threw the Jeep into drive and accelerated, leaving him standing on the street, returning my hand gesture.

Looking in the rearview mirror, I considered wheeling the car around and running him over, but again, assaulting a cop wasn't on my agenda for the afternoon.

Halfway downtown, my cell phone rang. I thought about ignoring it, sure it was Kendall, but when I looked, it was a number I didn't recognize.

"Marlie Windsor," I mumbled, trying not to sniffle into the phone.

"Ms. Windsor, this is Alan over at Big Al's Automotive. You just had your oil changed and you left something behind. We're going to be open for another hour or so, if you want to come back and pick it up."

"I'll turn around and be there in a few," I reported. "By the way, what did I leave?"

But he had already hung up.

Suspicion vibrated through my being. Maybe they were on to me? Had someone figured out I'd been listening in or I'd noticed the car exiting with something attached to the undercarriage? What could I have possibly left behind? I never got out of my vehicle. Maybe I should call Kendall?

To hell with Kendall, I thought angrily. I'd already solved two cases, why not a third one.

I pulled up front and entered Big Al's, all of my senses on high alert.

"I'm Marlie Windsor, I was told I left something behind?"

"Give me one minute," the girl behind the counter told me, giving me a dangerous look.

Glancing at her name tag, I realized this was the girl Allison, who had run out of the garage when Big Al had started yelling the other day. I guess the personnel changes we'd assumed were coming, hadn't taken place.

I watched her disappear into the garage. A young man with Alan on his shirt came in, smacking a familiar 1x2 about three feet long into his palm.

"We forgot to put this back under your hood. We can change those hood dampeners for you sometime if you'd like, then you could ditch the 1x2."

I swallowed nervously. "Thank you, I'll keep it in mind."

"Have a good evening, Ms. Windsor," Alan told me before disappearing back into the garage.

Taking the stick I used to hold my hood open, I got back into the 'Beast' and left Big Al's shop behind me.

I needed a plan. There was a shipment coming tonight and if it was drugs, I wanted to be the one to shove it in Kendall's face after our argument earlier.

Flipping a u-turn at Union and Platte, I pulled into the parking lot of the sleaze bag motel, the kind that rents rooms by the hour, across the street from Big Al's. Dialing up Kendall's number, I left a message explaining what I'd seen before our argument. He was probably ignoring my calls for all I knew.

11

I was on a stake out of my own, across the street at the grungy dive motel on Platte, my trusty binoculars in hand. I'd had to purchase a pair when I was following someone around during the Rose O'Brien case. It was an extremely grungy feeling, renting a room at this place. I'm sure it was a gem back in the 60's in its prime, but these days not so much.

Lifting my binoculars to my eyes, I gasped.

Damnit, what was he doing here already? I wondered, as I watched Kendall park out front. It was just after the close of business; the delivery was supposed to take place later tonight. Where was his backup?

Focusing in on him, I watched him flash his badge. The mechanic named Alan let him into the shop. Through one of the big garage doors I could see Allison appear and speak to Kendall.

"Kendall," I shouted out, just before Alan hit him with something from behind. Kendall dropped like a load of rocks. Alan grabbed him under the arms and dragged him out of sight.

Without stopping to think, I grabbed my cellphone and bolted across the street, cars blowing their horns at me as I dodged through the traffic.

There had to be a back door. Slipping along the west side of the building and around the dumpster, I stopped when I heard voices. I settled beneath the open window of the shop's office, the dumpster concealing me from the street. My heart pounded wildly within my chest. I thought I may have a heart attack at any moment, from the adrenaline flowing in my system.

"We gotta get rid of this cop," Allison grumbled.

"He's a cop, Allison. We can't," Alan's voice quavered. "I didn't sign up for this."

"Shut up and let me think," Allison commanded.

I didn't dare venture a peek inside the window. I waited and listened, not sure what exactly to do.

"I need to know what he knows," I heard Allison say. "Get a bottle of water from the fridge and dump it over his head."

I heard shuffling and a door opening.

“Damn cops,” Allison muttered. “Nice piece.”

As quietly as I could, I stood and pressed my back against the brick wall, casting a sideway glance through the window. From where I was, I could see everything inside the office reflected in a picture on the wall.

Kendall was in a chair, his arms bound behind him. Allison was admiring a weapon which I assumed she’d taken from Kendall. Alan came through the door and handed a bottle of water to Allison.

She unscrewed the plastic cap, tossing it on the floor behind her.

“Wakey, wakey,” she mocked, as she poured the water over Kendall’s head.

Kendall sputtered and shook his head, struggling against his restraints. “What the fu..?”

“Officer Kendall, is it?” Allison grinned, putting a foot on the chair between his legs and waving the 9mm in his face.

“Detective…Kendall,” he shot back indignantly.

"You're just too nosy for your own good, detective. But I need to know what you know or what you think you might know," she told him.

Allison turned to Alan, "Make sure he's not wired."

She backed away and Alan began frisking Kendall, patting him down through his shirt.

Wired? Pulling out my phone, I made sure it was on silent and then hit the button, turning the camera on and started filming.

"He's clean," Alan told her, tossing Kendall's phone to her.

"It's locked," she complained, before tossing it behind her onto the desk. She sat on the desk, clutching the edge, and leaning towards the boy child detective.

"So, detective, what brings you here this evening?"

"I had a couple of questions for your father."

"About?"

"Dax Rubens," Kendall answered.

"Ah yes, poor, naïve Dax. He didn't know what was best for him."

"He discovered you were running drugs out of here and wouldn't cooperate, so you killed him."

"Was that supposed to be a question, detective?" Allison responded.

"It wasn't a question. It was a statement of fact."

"And where did you get your *facts*?" Allison questioned. "Because they aren't at all correct."

"A witness came forward and told me what happened the night Dax was murdered. The garage was dark. He was in one of the bays, by himself. You approached him and when he said he wouldn't run drugs for you, you told him he didn't have a choice then you pushed him into the grease pit."

In the reflection, Allison cocked her head to the side. I could tell Kendall had struck a nerve.

The smirk.

"I see my witness is pretty damn accurate."

Jumping up from the desk, Allison backhanded Kendall, his head snapping to the left. He began to chuckle and turned slowly back to look at her.

Why was he provoking her like in such a manor?

"Your witness is mistaken. Dax didn't die because he didn't want to be involved with the drugs, he didn't care we were dealing out of the garage, though he refused to use them himself, being the star athlete that he was. He died because he wouldn't sleep with me. I always get what I want. But no, the little wimp was afraid of daddy and said he really loved his dumpy little blonde girlfriend," she sneered, disgust showing on her face. If I couldn't have him, then nobody else would either. Plus, there are no witnesses left, I've made sure they've all been silenced. Comes in handy to be a mechanic and make things look like an accident."

"What do you mean, Allison?" Alan piped up, suddenly finding his voice.

"Shut up, Grant!"

Grant? I thought his name was Alan.

Kendall turned toward him. "Why does your shirt say Alan if your name is Grant."

"It's Big Al's shop. We're all assigned names that begin with Al."

"I said, shut up," Allison screamed, waving the firearm around again wildly.

"No, Allison. What do you mean you silenced them and made it look like an accident? Did you kill Darryl too and make it look like his brakes failed?"

"The little wimp was starting to have second thoughts. Said I should confess to Dax's murder, said Dax was haunting his dreams."

At least I wasn't the only one he was haunting, I thought.

"Oh, my gawd, Allison."

"Don't you, oh my gawd, me, you little weasel. You'd have nothing if it weren't for me. My dad doesn't pay us enough to live on. Which is why we're doing all of this, remember. Do you think your wife and kid care where the money comes from?"

"You told me Dax fell."

"He did…" she smiled, "after I pushed him."

Forcefully, she shoved the gun up underneath Grant's chin.

"Looks like I'll have to dispose of you as well as the cop," she threatened.

Bingo! I had the evidence Kendall needed. Now I had to get him and Grant out of there before Allison made good on her threat.

Backing away from the window, I grabbed a chunk of asphalt which had broken loose from the edge of the driveway. I moved as quickly as I could to the front of the building and hurled the chunk through one of the panes of glass in the first garage door and ran.

I dashed about thirty yards down Platte and ducked behind the next building, then dialed 911.

"911, what is your emergency?" The dispatcher asked calmly.

"Officer needs assistance at Big Al's Auto on Platte. Det. Kendall is being held inside," I whispered out of breath from my sprint.

Up the street, I heard shots ring out.

"Shots fired," I yelled before hanging up.

I clutched my phone to my chest and prayed. *Please Lord, let Kendall be okay.*

I couldn't stand the uncertainty and rushed back towards the mechanic shop's open window. Hearing a voice, I approached with caution and snuck a glance inside.

Kendall, still tied to the chair, had toppled over. Grant stood over him with the 9mm in hand. Allison lay on the floor in a pool of blood.

"I need an ambulance at 3245 East Platte. Two people have been shot," Grant relayed into the cell phone at his ear.

Running around to the front of the building, I tried the door, expecting it to be locked. To my surprise, it opened with ease.

"I'm coming in, don't shoot," I hollered. "The police are on the way."

Easing towards the office, I waved a hand in the doorway.

"The gun is on the desk. I'm not armed," Grant relayed in a hushed tone.

Peeking around the corner, I saw Kendall was one of the gunshot victims. He'd taken a round to the left side of his abdomen. Not concerned with my own safety, I ran in and knelt next to the boy child detective.

"Ms. Windsor?" Grant said, recognizing me.

"You shouldn't be here," Kendall groaned.

Grant sat there as I rummaged around in the desk to locate something to cut the cord they had tied Kendall to the chair with. Grabbing a utility knife, I slipped behind him and sliced through the bonds.

"Too late," I replied, ripping open his blood-soaked shirt.

"I don't think it hit anything vital," he told me.

Pulling my shirt over my head, I used it to apply pressure to the wound. "I thought you were a cop, not a doctor. Don't you dare die on me, Kendall."

"How are you ever going to ask me out if I die on you?" He winked with a grin, taking in my unclothed torso.

"Not a word, or I stick my finger in your wound and drive the bullet in further," I warned, raising my finger up for him to see.

Sirens wailed in the distance, clearly moving in our direction.

"Guess I can't be too upset you ignored me on this one," he admitted. "Didn't suspect Allison, so they caught me flat-footed."

"Didn't you get my message? I saw a car leave with something hanging from the undercarriage. There is supposed to be a delivery tonight, so I was across the street at the sleaze bag motel, waiting for you to show up with the calvary, but you showed up with no backup," my words spilled out at an enormous rate.

"You were waiting for me in a motel?" He asked, a seductive tone to his question.

"All you got out of what I just told you, was I was waiting in the motel?"

"Well, I'm a guy."

I held up my index finger again, daring him to say another word.

He coughed out a light chuckle and then grimaced in pain. Suddenly the room was abuzz with people.

"We'll take it from here, ma'am," a paramedic told me, placing a hand on my shoulder.

"Hey, keep your hands off of my woman there, bud," Kendall teased.

"He's lost a lot of blood," I told the first responder, "so he's a little out of it."

I backed away, my hands glistening red with the boy child detective's blood.

As they wheeled him away, Kendall asked one of the cops on scene to take his keys and get me one of his shirts from the trunk of his car.

"Nice bra.. red is definitely your color," he chirped, knowing he was out of my reach.

After they loaded him into the ambulance, I found the washroom and cleaned the blood from my hands. It was surreal watching the scarlet water swirl down the drain.

The officer with whom Kendall had spoken, returned, and handed me a pale blue dress shirt, along with Kendall's keys.

"Wait," I stopped him, "I barely know the detective, you should keep these. I don't think he'd want me to have them."

I dangled the keys out in front of me, offering them back to him.

"I heard him call you, his woman. You can take them down to the hospital when you return his shirt," he replied with a wink.

It finally dawned on me, I was only partially dressed, and with all these people milling about the crime scene, I stood out like a sore thumb. Heat rose in my torso as I felt myself blush from the waist up.

"We'll also need you to make a statement," he called over his shoulder. "But you may want to put that shirt on first."

Like that was going to happen before I spoke with the injured detective, the statement, not the shirt.

Slipping my arms through the sleeves, my hands began to tremble as I fastened the buttons, the reality of the evening's events hitting me full force.

12

Kendall was sitting up in his hospital bed when I tapped lightly on the door. He opened his eyes and then rolled them.

"You look a helluva lot better than you did the last time I saw you," I teased.

"Thank you."

I held the blue shirt he had asked the officer on scene to get me. "I dropped in to return this *and* your car keys."

I placed his keys and the folded shirt on the chair by the window.

"You didn't make copies of my house keys, did you? Am I going to find you curled up on my bed in that t-shirt some night when I get home from work?"

"You really need to stop," I warned him with a controlled smile.

"Are you sure you didn't come to take advantage of me while I'm laid up?" He asked, giving me a sly wink.

"I'm going to give you a break because you're most likely on really strong pain meds, but no."

"I can slide over to make room for you," he patted the mattress. He leaned so far back he almost fell out of the opposite side on the bed.

Reaching out, I grabbed his arm to keep him from tumbling out of the other side.

"Whoa there, Nellie," I called out, pulling him back to a sitting position.

"You saved me again," he smiled, "are you sure you're not here to take advantage of me?"

I wanted to tell him he wasn't my type, but if he had been twenty or so years older, he'd definitely be my type, but here and now…nooooo. I shuddered at the thought.

"Come on, Marlie, you know you're dying to ask me out."

The slight slur to his words and the glossy sheen in his eyes confirmed he had some really great drugs flowing through his IV. Not gonna lie, I was kinda jealous.

"Dream on, Kendall."

He grinned lazily, his eyes struggling to remain open.

"I think it's exactly what I'm going to do, right now. I can hardly keep my eyes open," his eyes drifted shut. Within a few minutes, he was in lala land and breathing deeply.

My motherly instinct wanted to brush the hair from his eyes, but that would be all I'd need, for him to wake up and find me caressing his head. Or for Helen to just happen by. Aye yai yai. No thank you!

I watched the boy child detective sleep for a few minutes. Before leaving, I whispered softly, "Sleep well, detective."

Exiting Kendall's room, I glanced down at my watch, when I saw a pair of black pumps step in front of me.

"You again?" The voice was angry and sarcastic.

I knew whose voice it was. There before me stood, DA Victoria McAdams, her left eyebrow arched at a severe angle.

"He's sleeping," I informed her.

"What, are you his personal bodyguard now?" She chided.

"Well, I did save him from bleeding to death. And I kinda helped CSPD solve not one, not two… but three cases," I gloated, holding up my hand with three fingers extended.

"And what exactly were you doing at the crime scene anyway?" She asked, crossing her arms over her chest and glaring at me.

"Well, if the detective would have just listened to me, I wouldn't have been there at all, and he wouldn't have been shot. But that's another story for another day."

"I suppose it was another '*vision*' which immersed you in this investigation?" She used her fingers to make quote marks when she'd uttered the word vision.

"Wow, you're finally catching on," I offered in bitter retort.

"One of these days, Kendall is going to find out you're a fraud and I can hardly wait for that day to come," she told me through narrowed eyes.

"We'll see. One of these days, you're gonna need me and you're going to have to ask me for my help," I snipped, holding up an index finger and shaking it at her.

"It will be a cold day in hell before I ask for help from a charlatan like you," she sneered, squinting her eyes at me.

I gave her a smirk of my own, (feeling the satisfaction it must bring Kendall), then stepped around her.

"You should really let him sleep. I hope you have the day you deserve, Victoria," I whispered over my shoulder at her.

I had been waiting for years to be able to use that specific line on someone and Victoria McAdams was the perfect target.

****

After I'd chucked the piece of asphalt through the garage door, she and Grant had wrestled for Kendall's gun, the first wayward discharge struck Kendall in the side. The second had hit Allison in the shoulder and when she released the weapon, Grant had hit her over the head, knocking her unconscious.

Both Allison and Grant were charged with kidnapping, felony assault on a law enforcement officer, conspiracy, and distribution of a controlled substance. After a NIK test, it was determined they'd had been dealing cocaine out of Big Al's Automotive.

Alan, or Grant, I should say, cooperated fully with the authorities and made a plea deal for his testimony in Allison's trial.

Allison survived her gunshot wound and is awaiting trial in the El Paso County Jail. Along with the other charges, she was also charged with two counts of first degree murder in the deaths of Dax Rubin's and Darryl Smythe.

It turned out the 'shipment' was just that, a shipment of replacement auto parts. The driver of the delivery truck was so startled to see all the police activity at the garage, he pulled up and immediately pulled away, which was deemed suspicious, so he was stopped and detained. After a consensual search of the load he was hauling and with nothing being discovered illegally in the back of the trailer, the driver was subsequently released.

****

I couldn't bring myself to wear the Eagles 1974 Tour shirt knowing what had transpired while Dax was wearing it. I would just have to find alternative ways to dream about my man, Don.

An Interview with Det. Jace Kendall

There is a soft breeze blowing through the window of my office when I hear a rap upon my door. When I answer it, I am met by the boy child detective, Jace Kendall. He is dressed in a blue suit with a matching plaid tie and looking quite stylish and handsome this morning.

Author: Welcome back, Detective Kendall. Please.

I open the door further and invite him into my office. Once again, he sits in the armchair across from me.

Kendall: Thank you, it's nice to see you again.

Author: Likewise. Would you care for coffee or water?

Kendall: Water sounds good.

I take a glass from the counter and pour water from a filtered pitcher in the small refrigerator, and hand it to him.

Kendall: Thank you.

Taking a seat, I pull out a note pad to write down our conversation.

Author: I'm curious, you keep threatening Marlie with arrest. Would you really arrest her?

Kendall: Damn right I would. She gets herself into more trouble than anyone I've ever met. Part of my job is to serve and protect. I can't do my due diligence if she is always searching for trouble.

Author: You caught a break on this case.

Kendall: I did. I just had a gut feeling Dax Rubins had been murdered, but everything led nowhere. I literally could have kissed Ms. Windsor when she told me about the t-shirt.

Author: Ms. Windsor? I thought the two of you were on a first name basis now?

Kendall: I think I'm on a first name basis with her. She still calls me Kendall or Detective.

I stifle the urge to inform him of her habit of referring to him as The Boy Child Detective.

Author: The two of you appear to be getting along better.

Kendall: She's a pain in my ass, but I have to admit she sure saved mine this time. No telling where I'd have ended up had she not ignored me.

Author: Yeah, things could have gone much worse if she hadn't been staked out at the motel across the street.

A grin creeps across his face and I notice his chest move with a small chuckle.

Kendall: She sure doesn't like it when I accuse her of wanting to ask me out. I find it hilariously funny to watch her expressions when I bring it up.

Author: Well, as she has mentioned to others, she's old enough to be your mother.

Kendall: Honestly, she is more my dad's type than she is mine, but I sure enjoy giving her a hard time.

Author: So, she's like your mother?

Kendall: God, no. My mother is very prim and proper. You'd never find her under a car changing oil. Not that it's a bad thing. My mother is very dependent on her husband. Marlie seems to have this need to show everyone she doesn't need anyone. Least of all a man.

She doesn't need a man around to do all the manly things we're supposed to do.

He takes a drink from the glass.

Author: Were you truly upset with her when she obtained the information about Trent and Dax having an altercation prior to Allison pushing him into the grease pit?

He pauses briefly before he answers.

Kendall: Yes and no. I was grateful for the information, but she hasn't had proper training in police procedures. Like I told her, if the information isn't obtained legally then it could get the case dismissed. It's hard enough for the DA to work around Marlie's paranormal ability without having to reveal it in court.

Author: Which brings us back around to DA McAdams.

Kendall: Victoria is a sensible person. Most people wouldn't believe it if we told them about Marlie's visions when she wears something a murder victim wore. Hell, I didn't believe her in the beginning. But when you see it in action, there's no denying it.

Author: Would you ever consider using her abilities on cases you are already working?

Kendall: I would love to be able to use her abilities on cases, but I can't trust her to just do that part of the job. She always finds a way to involve herself in the case.

His cellphone rings and he looks at the screen.

Kendall: I have to take this. *He holds up a finger indicating I should wait for a moment.* Kendall. I'll be right there.

Hitting a button on the screen, he gives me a shrug.

Kendall: Duty calls.

Author: Thank you again, Detective. I look forward to speaking with you again in the future.

Kendall: I enjoy our chats.

The detective leaves to go work on a case. Somehow, I have the feeling he'll be back.

About the author:

Myrl V. Williams is a Colorado native and devoted mother, daughter, sister, and aunt. Like Marlie, Myrl lives in Colorado Springs with her adorable shih tzu, Laeto. Inspiration for Marlie's crazy exploits comes from family/friend stories and a file she keeps called 'Stuff My Sister Says', though the real title is slightly more colorful.

Her works include the Secondhand Homicide Whodunit series featuring Marlie Windsor, the If These Walls Could Talk series and an array of short stories.

The Secondhand Homicide Whodunit series developed after seeing a writing prompt on social media, she tweaked it to incorporate the cozy mystery vibe she felt upon seeing the prompt. As she began establishing the characters and setting, the entire story line erupted like 'Old Faithful'.

Email her at: authormyrlvwilliams@gmail.com

Facebook: https://www.facebook.com/MyrlVWilliams

Myrl V Williams

A Turn For the Worst

A Secondhand Homicide Whodunit (Book 4)

We descended from a brilliant blue, down into the gray haze of Los Angeles. The plane bounced hard upon landing, jostling any passengers who were still sleeping, fully awake. The young woman next to me gripped the armrest between us and made the sign of the cross over herself with her other hand, mumbling something in Spanish, which I didn't comprehend.

Exiting the aircraft, after waiting thirty-five minutes at the gate to disembark, we entered the monstrous complex of the Los Angeles International Airport or LAX, several passengers grumbling about missing connecting flights now.

Weaving in and out through the crowd, I made my way to baggage claim and waited for the conveyor to start its revolutions. I spotted my bag and waited for it to make the slow journey around to where I was standing. Struggling to get my luggage from the carousel, I nearly knocked the woman over who had sat next to me on the plane.

"I'm so sorry," I uttered apologetically, then "Lo siento," my limited Spanish surfacing from some small recess of my mind.

"Vieja perra torpe," she directed back at me with a scowl.

I opened my mouth in shock. I didn't know what 'torpe' meant, but I knew the meaning of 'perra' and 'vieja'. Vieja meant old. This young person was certainly not going to be considered my 'new best friend' after such a remark and 'perra' implied that I was a female canine.

She gave me a rude smile, collected her bags, and left me standing there, my mouth agape. I'd have to google 'torpe' when I got to my room, allowing me to expand upon my minimal Spanish vocabulary.

Recovering from my encounter, I stepped outside into the balmy, afternoon California heat and hailed a taxi. The smell of the ocean greeted me, and I closed my eyes to breathe in the salty air floating in from the

Pacific. My plans didn't include getting a rental car because everywhere I wanted to see was in walking distance from my hotel. If my plans changed, I'd just grab a ride from one of those transportation services or call for a cab.

Driving out of the airport, I looked for the historic Theme Building, scanning the horizon for the space-aged structure which looks like a flying saucer on four legs. The quintessential structure which serves as a landmark for LAX passed by on my left and I checked off an item on my bucket list.

After a daunting one-hour drive, from the airport to my hotel (through midday LA traffic), I checked in, dumped my bags in my room and headed out for my primary destination.

Tucked among all the posh boutiques of Rodeo Drive was a scant but whimsical secondhand shop called 'Hollywood Hand Me Downs'. Rumor had it that a plethora of well-known celebrities donated to this chic little establishment. I'd been itching to make the trip to LA to check it out, to see what the rich and famous tossed out and deemed charity worthy, curious as to what it had in store.

I was not disappointed. The place was small, but immaculately clean and very well organized. The owner, Rebecca, reminded me of my 8th grade French teacher, Ms. Scheibel, who always wore long flowing skirts, bangles on her wrists and leather sandals or boots; very Bohemian.

What the 'celebs' called used and had given away, was shocking. I guess when you have money to burn, you can choose to wear an outfit just one time and toss it away. Most of the 'rags' looked brand new, some still had the original tags on them, along with designer labels. Not being much of a fashionista, I sorted through the clothing racks quickly, selecting a few things I thought Helen, and my mother and sister might like.

Rebecca knew what a little goldmine she had, the prices weren't cheap, but they were reasonable.

There was an assortment of sunglasses, one pair claiming they were previously owned by JLo. No thank you, I'd had my fill of vintage spectacles, especially those blinged out cat-eye beauties from the 50's and 60's. I was more interested in the jewelry the rich and famous had cast out.

Each piece of jewelry was tastefully displayed, unlike most thrift shops where, many a time, the pieces were piled together in a tangled mess. My eyes fell upon a stunning strand of pale pink glass beads which I guessed to have been produced in the 1920's or 30's. I took them in hand, examining the craftsmanship of the necklace before me. I slipped them over my head. As soon as the cool beads hit my neck, I was no longer myself.

Knowing what was coming, I quickly pulled them from around my neck. I got that familiar, sinking feeling deep in the pit of my stomach. This wasn't the first time something like this had happened to me and I feared it wasn't going to be the last.

I'd been having visions of murder victims ever since I'd taken a blow to the back of the head a little over a year ago.

The middle of this Hollywood boutique was no place to bear witness to the vision I knew was held within the string of shiny glass beads, now clutched between my trembling fingers. No, I needed to purchase these and go back to my hotel, where I'd have some privacy. I'd once attempted to view a vision in the comfort of my car, only to have gathered an unappreciative audience, when I started waving my hands around at non-existent bees. One woman believed I was having a seizure and wanted to call 911.

Inquiring with the owner, as to the origin of the pink glass baubles, I learned the necklace had belonged to actress Astasha Bourne, who had died last year, after suffering a massive heart attack outside her apartment building here in Los Angeles.

I had to pay a pretty penny for the necklace, but it would be worth it in the long run. Not only would I be able to resell them once I returned home, but hopefully, I'd be able to find an answer to this woman's death in the meantime.

When I returned to the hotel, I took the stairs to the third floor, rather than the elevator, delaying what I had to do for as long as I could. Swiping my cardkey against the brass plate on the door, I entered my room in dismay.

"Why does this keep happening to me?" I groaned aloud, sitting at the edge of the bed, and placing the bag containing the necklace next to me.

It spilled out onto the floral bedspread, the light pink beads glistening in the fading sunlight peeking in through the window. With reluctance, I slipped them over my head once more.

I stepped into the revolving door of my apartment. God, how I hate this thing, I thought. I pushed and the door moved forward, only to come to a jarring stop. I pushed harder. I began throwing myself at the door, but it wouldn't budge. My heart started pounding faster, I could feel a panic attack beginning to build.

I screamed, hoping someone would hear my calls of distress. All it did was reverberate around the glass cage in which I found myself trapped. I began pounding on the thick pane only to find my reflection pounding back. But as I screamed once more, my reflection did not, it smiled wickedly back at me. *Sissy,* I thought, *sissy, help me.*

My pulse raced erratically; I could feel it hammering inside my head and pulsating within my veins.

Pain. Pain in my chest. I pressed my hand flat above my breasts, trying to catch my breath through the stabbing discomfort. My entire body felt as though it was seizing up on me. *Oh my God, where is Joe? I need Joe.*

I slid down the glass, clutching at my chest, wondering why Veressa wasn't helping me. I closed my eyes, never to open them again.

Pulling the beads from around my neck, I just sat at the edge of the bed. Thrice before this had happened to me. I was going to have to resign myself to the fact that this 'ability' didn't seem like it was going to end, and it was now a part of my life. I didn't relish this in the least.

I knew the face in the reflection of the glass of the revolving door. Astasha Bourne had been a rising star in Hollywood and had died from an 'apparent' heart attack a little over a year ago.

It was afterhours in Colorado, so I opted for a trip to Santa Monica and decided to call Kendall the first thing in the morning for his advice on how to proceed. No need to bother the boy child detective until tomorrow, Astasha Bourne wasn't going anywhere, and neither was her necklace.

The necklace had thrown a monkey wrench into my whole plan of not needing a car. I called for an INAR and asked to be dropped off at the pier in Santa Monica to enjoy an evening oceanside stroll, and contemplate my future and these visions.

www.ingramcontent.com/pod-product-compliance
Lightning Source LLC
LaVergne TN
LVHW010619100826
845148LV00014B/3039

* 9 7 8 1 7 3 6 4 8 3 0 4 6 *